Praise for Elaine Wolf's *Camp*:

"Blew my emotional socks off! *Camp* is a book that will stay with you long after you finish reading it."

—*Beth Fehlbaum, author of* Big Fat Disaster

"A moving and thoroughly absorbing coming-of-age tale. A good pick for mother-daughter book clubs, as the mother-daughter relationship is integral, and the themes of forgiveness and acceptance will resonate. I highly recommend it!"

—*Kirsten Lopresti, author of* Bright Coin Moon

"*Camp* is a great summer read. This book has many facets to it: relationships in families, secrets, bullying, courage and forgiveness. It's a very compelling book that makes you think about how complicated relationships can be when people keep secrets and the price is paid."

—*Youth Services Librarian, Howell Carnegie District Library (Michigan)*

"A beautifully written and important story about bullying and the complexities of the mother-daughter relationship that is a must read!"

—*mompopculture.com*

"A fascinating, emotional tale. A perfect addition to any reading list."

—*Tradina Demary, examiner.com*

"*Camp* is a classic coming-of-age tale that recalls the work of Judy Blume in her prime with its likable (and refreshingly "real") heroine. . . . *Camp* raises difficult topics . . . in ways that are always honest, direct, and never melodramatic."

—*Elizabeth Ridley, author of* Dear Mr. Carson *and* Rainey's Lament

"You know when you come across one of those books that really makes you stop and think about not only your life but the way the world is? A book that grabs you and shakes you down to your core. Shakes hard. It's rare, unique, and to be treasured. That is exactly what I found in *Camp*. Elaine Wolf deserves tremendous praise for her amazing talent."

—*UniquelyMoiBooks.com*

"Masterly written and delivers powerful and important messages."

—*keenlykristin.com*

"I refused to stop reading until I had finished *Camp*."

—*Nerdy Book Club*

"Read this book. Please. I give *Camp* five stars."

—*L. Gaines, teen book blogger at "Authoress in the Making"*

"I loved *Camp* so much that I am writing about it at three o'clock in the morning. There's something that will resonate with every reader. This is a story about the horrors of bullying, the bonds of family, the power of memory, and the strength that one can find in the most unlikely places. Get it now."

—*TheWriteTeachers*

"An excellent book for mothers and daughters to read together. I would definitely read Elaine Wolf again!"

—*I'dSoRatherBeReading.com*

"Reminded me of *A Tree Grows in Brooklyn* with survival instincts that brought to mind *Lord of the Flies*. Impressive character development makes Amy a character to root for, and *Camp* impossible to put down until you reach the final word."

—*ratherbereadingblog.com*

"*Camp* is definitely a book that should be read and discussed. It's intense, surprising, and chock full of emotion. It could easily be added to units on bullying and/or familial relationships."

—*YAloveblog.com*

"I loved this book and think it's suitable for all ages. It should be required reading in schools."

—*I'd Rather Be Reading At The Beach*

Awards and Recognition for *Camp*:

Book of the Month, Holocaust Memorial & Tolerance Center of Nassau County (New York)

Publishers Weekly Bullying Resources: A Selected Listing

Examiner.com's Top Ten YA Fiction

Arkansas Teen Book Awards Reading List grades 7–12

Top 10 Picks for Peters Township Teens (Pennsylvania)

Also by Elaine Wolf

Danny's Mom

CAMP

A Novel

Elaine Wolf

Sky Pony Press
New York

Copyright © 2012 by Elaine Wolf
First paperback edition, 2015

All Rights Reserved. No part of this book may be reproduced in any manner without the express written consent of the publisher, except in the case of brief excerpts in critical reviews or articles. All inquiries should be addressed to Sky Pony Press, 307 West 36th Street, 11th Floor, New York, NY 10018.

Sky Pony Press books may be purchased in bulk at special discounts for sales promotion, corporate gifts, fund-raising, or educational purposes. Special editions can also be created to specifications. For details, contact the Special Sales Department, Sky Pony Press, 307 West 36th Street, 11th Floor, New York, NY 10018 or info@skyhorsepublishing.com.

Sky Pony® is a registered trademark of Skyhorse Publishing, Inc.®, a Delaware corporation.

Visit our website at www.skyponypress.com.

10 9 8 7 6 5 4 3 2 1

The Library of Congress has cataloged the hardcover edition as follows:

Wolf, Elaine.
Camp / Elaine Wolf.
p. cm.
Summary: In 1963 at a Maine summer camp, fourteen-year-old Amy Becker is forced to face the camp bully, Rory, family secrets revealed by her cousin Robin, and worry about having to leave her mentally challenged brother with their cold, harsh mother.
ISBN 978-1-61608-657-2 (hardcover : alk. paper)
[1. Camps--Fiction. 2. Bullies--Fiction. 3. Mothers and daughters--Fiction. 4. Brothers and sisters--Fiction. 5. Secrets--Fiction. 6. Maine--History--20th century--Fiction.] I. Title.
PZ7.W81855165Cam 2012
[Fic]--dc23
2011047125

Cover design by Brian Peterson
Cover photo credit Shutterstock

Paperback ISBN: 978-1-63220-422-6
Ebook ISBN: 978-1-63450-028-9

Printed in the United States of America

*In loving memory of my mother,
whose story I can only imagine.*

Contents

"The past is never dead.
It's not even past."

William Faulkner,
Requiem for a Nun

"My parents' past
is mine molecularly."

Anne Michaels,
Fugitive Pieces

Chapter 1

I Hate Her

When I was fourteen, not quite four years ago, I'd lie awake at night and pray my mother would die.

If I had known her secret, I might not have hated her. But my parents didn't tell me about the ghost that slipped into the hospital the day I was born. It crept across my umbilical cord, linking me to my mother's past. Then it wedged right between us. My father said doctors couldn't explain the purple blotches on my chest. But now I'm sure of this: That phantom punched me hard. And though the black-and-blues faded before I could crawl, the ghost kept pushing my mother from me, flexing its muscles, bulking up. So by the time my parents sent me to sleepaway camp, that ghost was larger than I was. I just hadn't seen it yet.

●

Dad sprang the news about camp on us in the fall when I was in ninth grade. "I heard from my brother today," he announced at dinner as my mother carried a plate of lamb chops to the kitchen table. The smell of meat thickened the air. "Ed closed the deal on that girls camp he's been looking at."

My mother's hands shook on hearing Ed's name. Back then, in 1962, I couldn't have guessed the real reason my uncle rattled her, though I would find out in time.

"And there's great news for you, Amy," my father told me. He smiled so wide I saw his gold tooth. "Guess who's going to sleepaway?" Dad used his happy birthday voice, the tone usually followed by a brightly wrapped package.

But camp was a present I didn't want. What if all the girls knew each other from past summers? And how could I leave my little brother, Charlie? Who would play with him when he'd come home from summer school at The Woodland Center for Handicapped Children? Who would read to him while our mother made supper or brought the laundry up from the basement or mopped the bathroom floor?

"Dad, I don't want to go," I said flatly.

"You're not worried about the cost, honey, are you?" He kept talking before I could tell him that wasn't it—not at all. "'Cause everything's worked out already. I'll help Uncle Ed with the bookkeeping, and you'll go to camp for free. Isn't that great news?" My father lifted his water glass as if to toast me. "The two oldest cabins are for girls just your age."

My mother uncovered a pot. The lid clanged the stove. "Lou, you said we'd discuss this when the deal went through. We need to talk about it."

"We will. It'll be fine." My father faced me and smiled again.

"Dad, I really don't want to go." What if nobody liked me? I'd be all alone. Not even Charlie to talk to, to care for. I slid closer to him and jabbed a bite of meat. But when I held out his fork, my brother refused it. Instead, he drummed the table—a kind of frenzied patting.

"Don't be silly, Amy," my father said. "Of course you want to go. Who wouldn't want eight weeks by a lake in Maine?"

"Lou," my mother said once more, turning from the stove this time. She stared hard at my father, then fixed on Charlie. "I said we need to talk about this."

"But Ed says it's a beautiful place."

"What could Ed possibly know about running a camp?"

"Sonia, come on, Sonia. He'll learn. And the property's terrific. In great shape, Ed says."

"I don't care what Ed says."

"Why can't you just be happy for him? We're family, for God's sake. Brothers support each other. And anyhow, Ed got a good deal, and Amy gets to go to camp. What could be wrong with that?"

"I told you," my mother answered. "Ed doesn't know the first thing about running a camp."

"And I told you he'll learn. And he won't even have to change a thing. He already talked to the head counselor.

She's been there two or three summers, and she said she'll come back."

"Dad, I really don't think…" I placed a hand on Charlie's, stilling his fingers. Everything stopped: the air in the kitchen, the swish of my mother's spoon in the vegetable pot, the questions in my mind.

"Your mother's right, Amy. Right as usual. She and I will talk about this later."

I forced a playfulness into my voice then, a reassurance for myself as well as for Charlie that nothing would change, that no one would go away for the summer. "Let's pour some ketchup, buddy. Then you can dip, okay?"

My mother turned a thimbleful of peas onto Charlie's plate. He grabbed his fork, holding it tight in his scrawny fist. "No." Charlie mustered up his gravelly voice. "No. No!" He swiped at his plate, sending meat and vegetables through the kitchen.

My mother leaped up behind him, her hands heavy on Charlie's birdlike shoulders.

"It's okay, son," my father said, as Charlie struggled to twist loose, his eyes finding mine.

"Mom, let him go!" The words spilled from my mouth. I couldn't stop them, though I knew I'd get in trouble. "Please, Mom. You're hurting him." I looked to my father in silent pleading: *Do something.*

My mother's eyes burned into me. "You think you're so smart, Amy? You know what's best for your brother? Then *you* make him behave."

"Please," I tried again, my voice softer now. "Just let him go, Mom."

"Oh, you don't know anything, Amy," she said. Charlie wriggled faster to escape our mother's grip. "You don't know anything. Nothing."

"But you're hurting him!" I tried once more, my courage fueled by anger. How dare she treat Charlie like that. "Stop squeezing his shoulders!"

My mother shot Dad a look. "Don't you tell your mother how to manage her own son, young lady," my father said.

Charlie finally freed himself and flew from the kitchen. I followed my brother up the stairs, pounding the steps to the beat in my mind: *I hate her. I hate her. I wish she were dead.*

I hated how my mother made my father buckle. I hated how my mother treated Charlie. I hated how she made me feel unworthy of her love.

That night my father told us about camp, I prayed my mother would die.

Chapter 2

The Requirement of Perfection

The day before camp started, my mother and I went to Woolworth's for the toiletries I hadn't packed in my trunk: a soap holder, collapsible plastic cup, Prell shampoo. When an extra dollar popped up on the cash register, my mother tapped her foot, ticking off seconds while the checkout girl struggled to cancel the overcharge. My mother glanced at her watch. Charlie's bus was due at the house in twenty minutes.

"Sorry, ma'am," the cashier said. "I need the manager."

"What's your name, young lady?"

"I'm trying my best, ma'am."

My mother sighed loudly enough for the clerk to hear, then asked again, "What's your name?"

I wished I could shrink to dime size and slide right into the register. Why did my mother always make a fuss over every little thing?

"Anna," the cashier mumbled, head down.

"What did you say?" The edge vanished from my mother's voice.

"Anna," the girl repeated, looking up now.

My mother let out a slow breath. "I'm sorry, dear." I barely recognized my mother's voice, suddenly so filled with softness I wondered what I had missed. Had my mother met this Anna before?

I recognized her as one of the girls I had seen on line at the Dairy Queen when my father and I took Charlie for a cone. When my brother spotted a dachshund, leashed at the far corner, Charlie's scream had silenced even the high school boys.

Now I smiled at the Woolworth's cashier—a thin smile of apology for my brother, my mother, and for simply being there at the five and ten. "Don't worry, Mom," I said as I studied the items I'd carry up to camp. "We've got a few extra minutes. Charlie's bus is always late on Fridays."

"I know that," she said. Unwilling to admit she forgot the details of his schedule, my mother looked in her change purse as if his program lined it. How could she have failed to remember? My mother mastered schedules the way she mastered cleaning. I used to wonder what went through her mind when she fluffed the pillows on the living room sofa as if company were coming, though rarely anyone came.

●

The alarm clock rang at six-thirty on the morning I left for camp. My eyes filled with tears as I memorized my room—the Russian nesting dolls on my dresser; Puppy, my oldest stuffed animal; my miniature porcelain dogs on the shelf by my bed.

Before Charlie was born, I had asked for a real dog. But my mother said she had enough to clean without pet hair. "And anyhow, dogs don't belong in a house," she announced, her tone ending discussion. "In Germany," she had said, "no one brought their dogs inside."

Now I rearranged my china ones, then got dressed in green shorts and a yellow shirt—my outfit for the next eight weeks. Yuck! Looking in the mirror, I saw someone you would pass without notice. Invisible except for that pathetic camp uniform. Not pretty like my mother. Not sexy like the popular girls in school. Just plain Amy Becker, disguised as a teenager whose parents could afford to send her to Maine for two months. How could I possibly be expected to wear this fitted T-shirt that hugged my chest, the Camp Takawanda logo a bull's-eye on my left breast?

And how would Charlie survive a whole summer without me to run interference between him and our mother? I had never left Charlie for more than a day, when I would sleep over at my friend Danielle's house. But even that ended when she got angry because I always had to stop what we were doing to call home at Charlie's bedtime. "Jeez, Ame," Danielle finally said, "aren't you ever gonna have your own life? I mean, shoot, your brother's gotta grow up sometime."

Danielle didn't understand why I had to say good night to Charlie. If I didn't, he wouldn't go to bed. Yet when I did, I had to remind Danielle that my brother was eight going on four. And I had to explain why I never invited Danielle to sleep over at my house. I couldn't even ask her to stay for dinner. Charlie, whose body barely took up space, filled the entire house. There was no room for outsiders.

If Danielle didn't understand that, well then, I'd be fine without her. Like my mother, I see now, I had learned to shut the outer world out, lock the inner world in. Was that how she survived when she left Germany? Growing up, I knew nothing of her life there. "Your mother doesn't talk about that," my father warned.

●

Charlie and I were in his room when my mother called us to breakfast. His carpet prickled my bare legs as I reached over to hand him a triangular wooden block to top the tower we'd built. I hadn't even left, and already I despised those skimpy green shorts and Camp Takawanda for Girls.

Charlie gripped the block and looked at me. I pointed to our building. "Come on, buddy. Put it up there." Charlie didn't move. "You have to stand to finish this." His blue eyes glazed when I smiled at him. "You know I'm going away today, don't you?" I rumpled his soft brown hair. "But you're gonna visit me in a month. And at the end of the summer, I'll be right back here with you."

"Amy! Charlie!" my mother called again from the bottom of the stairway. "I said breakfast is ready." Her harsh German accent made me flinch, each word a bullet from the back of her throat.

"We'll be right down," I answered as I studied my brother. "Come on, Charlie. You put that block on top, and then how 'bout we take a picture?"

Charlie jumped up, flapping his arms as if they were wings.

I pulled the Instamatic, which I had given Charlie for his last birthday, from its place on the third shelf. I'd gotten the idea when a Kodak ad leaped out of *Life* magazine: a fragile boy, no bigger than my brother, with a camera pressed to his eye and a grin filling his face. *Charlie could do that*, I thought. In my head, I saw us roaming the neighborhood, snapping away: Mrs. Harris's flower garden; the Anderson twins on their matching red bikes; even Zeus, the Sparbers' black Lab that darted down the block every time sixteen-year-old Mike opened the door to let friends in. The week before I bought the camera, Zeus had raced toward Charlie, who screamed until bedtime. Maybe if we caught Zeus on film, I thought, Charlie wouldn't be scared anymore.

Now on the day I left for camp, I looked through the camera, which my brother never used. I snapped a shot of Charlie standing by our tower of blocks.

"Let's go, kids!" Dad called. "Mom's making French toast."

"Okay, buddy," I said. "Clean up time. Ready?" Charlie knocked down the blocks, which I stacked on his two lowest shelves. First the large rectangles, then the smaller ones, and finally the squares and triangles. Everything in its place, and a place for every thing.

But why this requirement of perfection — those stupid rules that governed our lives?

●

A light blue apron, tied with a perfect bow, shielded my mother's navy dress as she stood by the stove.

"Sure is a hot one already," my father announced when he came to breakfast. "Think I'll turn on the living room air conditioner. Maybe a little air'll get in here."

"We'll be gone before it cools off," my mother answered. Her high heels, the exact shade of her dress, clicked the linoleum as she lay forks on the kitchen table.

I drizzled syrup on Charlie's French toast. "Don't let that get on his shirt," my mother said. "I don't want to have to change him before we go."

Why don't you just tell him to be careful? I almost screamed. *Why do you treat him as if he can't understand?* But the last time I talked back, my father followed me right into my room. "She's so mean!" was all I said before he started in: "I don't *ever* want to hear you talk about your mother like that!" His anger made me shudder. "She's had a really hard life, Amy." Silence for a moment. Then, his voice gentler, "I wish you could know what she's been through. Maybe someday you will."

That morning I left for Takawanda, I didn't talk back. I simply tucked a napkin into Charlie's shirt and said, "He won't get dirty, Mom. We've got it under control. Don't we, buddy?"

Charlie grabbed his fork and twirled it in the syrup.

"So today's the big day." My father's happy birthday tone seemed forced. "That uniform looks nice on you, honey."

I hunched to shrink the camp logo on my chest.

"Sit up straight, Amy," my mother ordered. "And watch your posture this summer. You're getting round-shouldered already."

"Sonia, please, Sonia. Can't we have one peaceful meal before she leaves?"

"She'll be old before her time if she doesn't watch her posture."

I stabbed a piece of French toast and tried not to sound teary. "May I be excused?"

"Excused? You haven't eaten anything," my mother said. "And please, Amy, sit up straight."

The camp logo rode high on my breast as I uncurled my spine. "But I'm not hungry, and Uncle Ed said we're eating on the bus."

"I don't care what your Uncle Ed said!"

Charlie started to tremble.

"Sonia, please," my father tried again. "It's a big day for her." He turned to me. "You nervous, honey?"

"A little."

"Well, no need. Why I'll bet you make so many friends you won't even want to come home."

Now Charlie's whole body shook. "It's okay, buddy," I said, placing a hand on his knee, then poking at a bite of French toast.

"You'll have a great time, Ame." My father spoke too loudly, as if trying to convince us.

My stomach knotted when I held the fork to my mouth. "Don't play with your food," my mother said.

I searched for an excuse to leave the table. "I have to go check my room. I need to make sure I didn't forget anything."

"What could you forget?" my mother asked. "We had a list."

True enough. She had ticked off the items as I laid them in my trunk. Four pairs of shorts. Check. Ten pairs of underpants. Check. Two bathing suits. Check.

When the packing was done, she had placed the camp list in that metal box in her closet—the box in which I saw her put Charlie's progress reports. The box where I assumed my mother stowed all those papers she took care of: birth certificates and vaccination records; school notes and clothing receipts.

I caught my father's eye across the table. "Go ahead," he said. "You're excused."

"No she's not. She hasn't eaten yet. She doesn't know how lucky she is to have a good breakfast." My mother's variation on *starving children in China*. The long version went like this: You don't know what it's like to be hungry and wonder where your next meal is coming from when you've left home in a hurry and you're all by yourself.

A clue to my mother's past. I had heard it so many times that I didn't even pay attention anymore.

"Go ahead, Ame," my father said again. Charlie pushed back his chair. "Go on now, both of you." My anxiety must have been visible: My father was risking my mother's fury to help me. I avoided her eyes as I left the kitchen, shadowed by Charlie, who followed me upstairs.

"You wait in your room, buddy," I said at the door to mine. I needed a moment to myself, a chance to breathe without reprimand or interruption. "I'll be there in a minute."

Charlie wrapped himself around my leg.

"I know. I wish I didn't have to go away today." I kissed the top of his head, then disengaged his arms. "But you go ahead now. Scoot." I gave him a playful nudge. "Scoot, scoot, skedaddle."

"Scoot, scoot, skedaddle," Charlie whispered, running the heels of his hands over his eyes.

I shut my door and opened my Russian nesting dolls to line them up on the dresser. The next-to-the-smallest doll stuck, trapping the tiniest one inside. I held Puppy to my face and inhaled my stuffed animal's peanut butter scent.

●

A half hour later, we were in the car—Charlie and I in the back of the brown Impala, our parents up front. A warm breeze whipped my face when my father rolled down his window. I grabbed a rubber band from the bag at my feet and pulled my hair into a ponytail.

"Well, at least one of us won't sweat to death all summer," my father said, raising his voice over the whoosh of passing cars. "I hear the weather's perfect in Maine. You're one lucky girl."

Lucky? Then why was my stomach doing somersaults?

I reached over to calm Charlie. His legs jiggled on the tan seat as we bounced along a road pitted with potholes. My mother inched forward with every bump.

"Sonia, for God's sake, Sonia. Relax," my father said.

"If she misses the bus, then what? We're driving to Maine?"

"Of course not. Helen's riding with the girls. She won't let the buses leave till everyone's accounted for."

My mother stayed quiet for a while after that, perhaps thinking about Aunt Helen and Uncle Ed. I don't know why, but I thought about last year's Thanksgiving dinner, when Aunt Helen told my mother, "It would be nice if we could come to your house for the holiday sometimes, Sonia. But I guess it makes more sense doing it here, what with our place being so much bigger. And anyhoodle, Thanksgiving's not really your holiday...I mean...well, it's not really part of your background, it being an American holiday and all."

"Who cares if we go to Aunt Sonia's?" my cousin, Robin, mumbled. "She can't even cook."

"Watch it, young lady," Uncle Ed warned his daughter. He caught my mother's eye and winked.

I wondered if Robin had seen what I had. All through dinner her father seemed to study my mother, as if his eyes could peel the dress from her slender body, leaving my mother naked at the table. Is that why she hurried out to the car with Charlie while my father lingered on good-byes? My father in his too-large pants and worn brown cardigan—so different from Uncle Ed, in a crisp sport shirt and sharp khaki slacks. Robin too must have noticed the contrast, or so I imagined she did.

Now I pictured my cousin as my parents, Charlie, and I drove in silence toward the Triborough Bridge—toward the camp bus—the only sound in the car the popping up and down, up and down of Charlie's legs as his skin kissed the vinyl seat.

"Sit still," my mother commanded.

I leaned over to quiet him.

"You never know what might happen to children who call attention to themselves," she went on. "Children should be seen and not heard." Another rule not to be questioned.

I stroked Charlie's legs and prayed that Robin and I wouldn't be in the same cabin. I hadn't said anything to my father about that. How could I have explained why I didn't want to be with my only cousin? How could I have told my father that Robin's vanity table with assorted makeup and hair rollers made me wish I could disappear?

"Setting and teasing your hair will just make it fall out," my mother had said in Woolworth's when I begged for rollers. "If you took better care of your hair, you wouldn't have to worry about setting it."

Now my mother spoke again as we crossed the bridge from Queens to Manhattan. "Amy, if they serve sweets at camp, don't eat too many." Her back stayed rigid as she shifted in her seat to glimpse over her shoulder. "It's a lot easier putting on weight than taking it off."

"Yes, I'll watch what I eat," I answered, wondering what camp food would be like.

My mother faced forward again but kept talking, pushing her voice over the clacking of tires on the metal joints of the bridge. "And go easy on the starches too. You'll never have a boyfriend if you gain weight."

"Well now, your mother's an expert on that, on keeping herself in shape," my father said, a smile in his voice. I noticed his arm move, his hand creeping across the front seat. "I mean, don't you agree she's the prettiest mom? No middle-age spread for her."

I didn't answer, just looked over at Charlie, who stared at the cars snaking toward toll booths.

"I'll tell you this, Ame," my father kept on, lowering his voice as bridge traffic slowed, "I guarantee your mother'll be the best-looking woman at the bus. It's no wonder your Aunt Helen's jealous."

"Lou!" My mother jerked up tall.

"But it's true. The way you always put yourself together, why I bet it makes Helen crazy. And Ed...well, he still goes nuts when he looks at us. I mean, really, he was the one who always scored with the girls. But look which brother won first prize."

"Enough, Lou!"

"What? Amy's not old enough to know these things?"

I made a fist, used my other hand to hold it on my lap. Why did my father always bring up Uncle Ed? Didn't he see that every time we visited his brother's family, my uncle hugged my mother too long, too close?

"Amy knows about those girls on Flatbush Avenue." My father wouldn't stop. "She knows about the stickball games and all the girls who came to watch Eddie."

"Some good that did him," my mother said. "Look who he ended up with."

"See, it's like I always say, Ame. I'm the lucky one. So listen: Whatever your mother tells you about what to eat at camp, you pay attention. 'Cause in the looks department, your mother sure knows what she's talking about." My father tapped his fingers on the steering wheel. I waited for him to start whistling, but we drove in silence through the city, through Central Park.

We pulled up in front of the Museum of Natural History to a jumble of campers, parents, and baggage. The other moms dripped sweat—despite sleeveless blouses and Bermuda shorts. Why did my mother always have to stand out? Mom in her navy dress with matching shoes.

But when I took in the campers, my mother's outfit didn't matter. Nobody was wearing the Takawanda uniform—except the seven-year-olds. Everyone else had on Saturday going-to-the-movie clothes: dungarees with short-sleeve blouses or Bermudas with madras tops. The oldest girls strutted in pedal pushers and shirts knotted at the waist.

"Hey, Amy!" Cousin Robin waved with both arms. "Over here."

I tried to smile, then studied the pavement. I wanted to slink into a crack when the laughter started. It floated above the whoops of campers reuniting, over the horns on Central Park West, over Charlie's whimpering as my father pulled him along.

"Go ahead, Amy," my mother demanded. "Go meet the girls."

"But they're all in regular clothes," I said to the ground.

"Go on, honey," my father prodded. The exasperation in his voice made me feel responsible, somehow, for not having known the dress code. "I told you, you look real nice in that uniform."

"But I didn't even pack other clothes. The instructions said uniform only. Mom said I couldn't bring anything that wasn't—"

"Ed should have told us she could wear something that wasn't on the list," my mother cut in. "Or Helen could have called."

"Well, it's too late now," Dad said. "So go on, Amy."

"But Dad…"

"Hold still!" he ordered Charlie, who squirmed to free himself from my father's grip. "And you, young lady, go meet your new friends. We'll be right here. We won't let you leave without saying good-bye."

Charlie twisted his skinny body. "I'll be back in a minute, buddy," I said, stroking his matted hair. "You wait here."

"No." Charlie bucked against my father. "No!" he screamed. "No! No!"

My mother took a step back from us. I heard her purse click open, the clinking of keys, the sound of a lipstick hunt. "I told you we should have left him home, Lou. The sitter was available. I told you that."

My father clutched Charlie's shoulder. "Son, settle down now, son. Nothing to get worked up about." Charlie wriggled to slip from his grasp. "I mean it!" My father's voice grew sterner.

"It's okay, buddy. I'm right here." I spoke softly, hoping to soothe Charlie. From behind, my mother said, "Here." She had fished a package of Charms from her purse.

I pulled out a red candy square as Aunt Helen barreled through the crowd. "It's all right, folks," she called, peering at me in my uniform. Her naked arms jiggled on approach. "Nothing to get excited about."

Aunt Helen stood in front of us. She scrunched her fists and planted knuckles on wide hips. In brown Bermuda shorts, she looked like a baked potato, all pasty and stuffed. "Just a little brother who doesn't want his sister to leave," Aunt Helen went on. "Isn't that right, Charlie?" She patted his head as if he were a dog, then looked at my father. "Why'd you bring him, Lou?"

Charlie struggled to turn away. "Everything's okay now, son," Dad said, using a soft voice this time to calm Charlie and, I suppose, to stop Aunt Helen's attack. Still clamping

Charlie's shoulder, he gave his sister-in-law a half-hug and an air kiss. My mother moved forward in family unity.

"Sonia," Aunt Helen said with a nod.

"Helen."

"We could have avoided this, you know," Aunt Helen said, drilling her eyes into my mother. "Lou could have brought Amy, and you could have stayed home with Charlie. Frankly, I don't know what you were thinking, Sonia, bringing him here this morning."

My father must have loosened his grip. Charlie slid out and attached himself to my leg. I popped the candy into his mouth as I heard cousin Robin and her new friends laughing.

Aunt Helen turned toward them and megaphoned her hands. "We'll be getting on the buses in a minute," she broadcast from her post, just inches in front of my family. "Our head counselor's comin' around to see that all the New York and Jersey campers are here. So parents, start your good-byes." Aunt Helen lowered her hands, then blared without assistance, "And it'll be easier on the girls if you make it fast. No need to hang around till the buses pull off."

"Oh, now she knows what's easier on the girls?" my mother whispered to no one.

"Sonia, enough, Sonia," my father said.

Charlie squeezed my leg. I looked down and touched his arm. "Listen, buddy. I have to get on the bus in a minute, but you're gonna be fine. And remember, you're coming to visit me in four weeks. And I'll send you lots of letters. Dad will read them to you." Charlie squeezed harder.

"Amy?" A voice I didn't recognize.

I looked up as a blond, ballerina-type woman approached. "You must be Amy Becker."

Charlie eased at the softness in the stranger's voice.

"Yes, I'm Amy."

In plain black Bermudas and a white sleeveless blouse, the woman looked like a Breck shampoo girl with an Ivory soap glow. "I'm Nancy, the head counselor. And let me see…" She crouched and placed her clipboard on the ground. "You must be Amy's brother," she said without rising. "It's a pleasure to meet you, young man."

"His name's Charlie," my father said, as Nancy gathered her clipboard and stood. "And I'm Lou. Lou Becker." He extended his hand.

"Nancy Logan."

"And I'm Mrs. Becker."

"Yes, of course. Amy's mother. I'm delighted to meet you. And don't you worry about your girl here. Takawanda's a great place. Amy'll have a terrific time." Nancy smiled a promise of support before she spoke to me again. "Sorry you didn't have a chance to meet the other seniors, but you'll meet everyone soon enough. So say good-bye. Then hop on that second bus over there."

"Sure thing." I tried to sound joyful, though Charlie wove an arm around my leg again. How could I say good-bye to him?

"Mr. and Mrs. Becker, I'll see you on visiting day." Nancy smiled once more, this time at Charlie, who didn't look up. "And Charlie, I'll see you then too, I hope."

My father pulled him from me, held him by the hand. No struggle. No screaming. Good, I thought. No problem.

I hugged Dad first. "I'll miss you so much, honey," he said. "But I want you to have lots of fun. And don't worry about things at home. Just have a great time. You deserve it. I love you."

"Thanks, Dad." I choked back tears. "I love you too."

I let go of my father and looked toward the buses. A few stragglers in uniform by the first one, Nancy hurrying them along. By the second bus, no one. They all must be on, I figured, waiting for me. "Time to go, Amy," Nancy called. "I'll be on the other bus. See you at the first rest stop."

Heads popped out of the Bus 2 windows. Senior campers craning for a show, I figured. I warned myself not to give them one. Just quick good-byes, then turn and go.

My mother was easy, barely a hug. "Have a good summer, Amy." She stood there, stiff as an oak. "We'll see you on visiting day."

For a moment, I felt nothing. But then I looked at Charlie and my heart thumped. "Okay, buddy. I love you." My voice broke. *Don't cry*, I told myself. *Don't make a scene.* "I'll see you on visiting day. Just four weeks," I whispered, hugging him.

"No!" Charlie screamed. "No! No! No!" Bloodcurdling loud like when Zeus, the Sparbers' dog, raced toward him. And over Charlie's shrieks, the laughter of girls.

"Just go, honey." My father grabbed Charlie's arm, then held him from behind. "He'll be fine."

"Go ahead," my mother said. "Get on the bus."

"I love you, buddy," I told Charlie again as I picked up my carry-on.

•

Aunt Helen sat up front, a grocery bag beside her. "It's about time, Amy."

I moved to the back of the bus, to the one empty seat by an oversized first-aid kit.

We pulled away. The girls ignored me. Or maybe I just didn't notice them turning in their seats to stare.

What I saw in my mind was my brother's face against the backdrop of cars on the Cross Bronx Expressway. How would he survive without my protection? And what about bedtime? I wouldn't be able to call. My mother had shown my father and me a letter Uncle Ed had sent to parents. I pictured it neatly folded and now safeguarded, I was sure, in my mother's metal box. *Camp is a self-contained environment*, the letter began, and then continued:

> *The sudden intrusion of the home world into*
> *the camp world can upset a camper's mind-set,*
> *causing a collision of two realities normally*
> *separated by time and distance. It's hard to*
> *adjust and reenter each world. Please respect that*
> *separation. Do not call.*

"How did Ed become such an expert?" My mother had asked before grabbing the paper back. "He buys a camp, and now he's a psychologist?"

"He got that letter from the Camping Association," my father said. "So why can't you give him credit for a change? I don't understand it. You and Ed used to get along so well."

I waited for my mother to send me to my room so she and my father could argue. I would hear it, as I usually did, from my perch on the top step: my mother complaining that Uncle Ed always brags about his business deals, and my father countering with pride in his brother's success.

But the night my mother showed us that letter, she didn't send me upstairs, and she didn't fight. All she said was, "Yes, Lou, we all used to get along. But that was a long time ago."

●

I shifted in my seat on the camp bus to avoid the first-aid kit. The girls started singing:

> A *hundred bottles of beer on the wall.*
> A *hundred bottles of beer.*
> If *one of those bottles should happen to fall,*
> Ninety-nine bottles of beer on the wall.

I willed Charlie to quit flapping in my mind as I sang quietly, hoping to blend my voice with those of the other girls. I wanted to be part of them, though I already knew I didn't want to be like them, showing off attitude like a new pair of Pappagallo shoes. But I was fourteen. I needed them to like me.

I sang louder and smiled at the thought of a summer without my mother. A memory played in my head—a day not long after Charlie was born. I pictured myself on Dad's lap in the armchair where he read from *The Tall Book of Fairy Tales*. I recalled the warmth of Dad's arms around me and the woodsy smell of his aftershave. *Merrily, merrily, do as you're told. Spin away, spin away. Straw into gold!*

"Feet please," my mother says, attacking the carpet and *Rumpelstiltskin* with a push. "I have to get in here."

"No, Mommy. Not now."

My mother turns off the vacuum. "Go to your room, Amy," she orders. "And stay there until I finish cleaning the house."

My father shoves me off his knee. "Do as you're told, Amy. And don't you *ever* talk back to your mother."

Now, at least, I'd have eight whole weeks without her. Maybe camp wouldn't be so bad after all. But what about Charlie? I'd write to him every day, I decided. I'd say that the smartest and prettiest and most popular girls saved a seat for me at the table and chose me for their team. My mother would get the letters first. And my father, all puffed up from sending me to paradise by the lake, would read them aloud—one each night—before Charlie would drift off. He would learn to sleep without my good night. He would have to.

Another song ended as a pigtailed redhead with a face full of freckles turned and smiled from across the aisle, several rows in front of me.

"Erin, what the hell do you think you're doing?" The redhead snapped around at this question from the girl behind her. "Now listen, all of you," that same camper continued. "Stay away from the new girl till after her initiation."

Initiation? Oh my God! What would they do to me? And why were they talking to cousin Robin? She was new too. Why no initiation for her?

"Whatever you say, Rory," a voice called from up front. "The new girl shouldn't even be here. She belongs with the kids in uniforms." Laughter filled the bus with darts aimed at me. I squeezed my eyes tight and longed to fade away. *Don't cry*, I told myself for the second time that morning.

I prayed Aunt Helen would make them stop. But she didn't say anything until a package of Hydrox cookies snaked from camper to camper. Then Aunt Helen boomed, "One each, girls. We want everyone to get some."

Only a few cookies remained when the package reached the redhead. Erin shifted around again, ignoring that bossy girl, Rory, and stretched across and back to give me a treat.

"Erin, what's the matter with you?" Rory barked.

Cookies slid to the edge of the wrapper as Erin held them out to me in silence.

"No thanks," I whispered, my refusal coming not from my mother's warning about sweets but from the queasiness in my belly. I tried to smile. "But thanks for offering."

Erin pulled the package back as Rory's arm jutted into the aisle. Cookies tumbled to the floor. "See what happens when you don't listen?" Rory said.

Her speech stopped all conversations. I knew I'd have trouble with her, though I never could have guessed how much.

●

Nancy saw me at the end of the bathroom line at the first rest stop. "Amy, hi," she called, clipboard in hand. "Have you met everyone?"

"Don't you worry, Nancy," Rory answered from several places in front of me. "We're welcoming her all right."

Nancy sidled beside me and rested a hand on my shoulder. "You doing okay?" she asked softly, inviting confidences.

I didn't see where Erin came from, but there she was, zooming in behind me. "Not to worry, Nance," Erin said quietly. "I'll take care of her."

"Thanks, Erin," Nancy said. "I knew I could count on you. And now you ladies will have to excuse me. I've got to supervise lunch for the younger girls. Can't let Jody do all the work over there." Nancy motioned to the Bus 1 campers, sliding onto picnic benches on the other side of a narrow road. A small woman dressed like Nancy—same black Bermudas, same white shirt—scattered bag lunches on wooden tables propped on sparse grass. "You'll meet Jody later, at camp," Nancy told me. "She's our head tennis counselor. Do you play?"

"Actually, yes. It's my favorite sport. So why don't I go over there and meet Jody now? I could help with the younger kids."

"Bad idea," Erin said, then lowered her voice to a whisper, as if suddenly aware someone might catch her talking to me. "Don't even think about it."

Nancy patted my arm. "That's very thoughtful. But Jody and I will have those little ones settled down in two shakes. And you seniors'll be boarding again in a minute. Not enough picnic tables. You get to eat on the go."

●

"Peanut butter and jelly or bologna?" Aunt Helen dipped into cartons on the ground by the bus and pulled out a lunch for each of us as we got back on. "And no changing seats now, girls. Just sit where you were so we can get this show on the road."

"Anything to drink, ma'am?" I heard Rory ask, her words drenched with respect now.

"Of course, dear. Once everyone's in, you'll get drinks." My aunt scanned the campers waiting to get on. "And please, everyone call me Aunt Helen. We're family for the summer."

Erin stood in front of me, but she didn't turn around. She hadn't spoken since her warning in the bathroom line. Rory had made it perfectly clear: no conversations until after my initiation.

I said the word to myself and swallowed hard. *Initiation. Initiation.* I shivered despite the heat.

Chapter 3

Boys on the Brain

My first letter from camp set the pattern for the start of that summer. The big lie: Camp is great. If I had told the truth, my mother would have said it was my fault, and my father would have felt guilty for sending me.

Dear Mom and Dad,

This is my "meal ticket." Patsy (my counselor) has to collect our letters at the end of rest hour, and anyone who doesn't have one won't be allowed into dinner. But I really want to write to Charlie, so I'll put all the news in his letter. Please read it to him before he goes to bed.

Love,
Amy

Dear Charlie,

It took so long to get to camp. I felt like we were on that bus for two days, but it was only about seven hours. I thought of you the whole time. I miss you, buddy!

I'm in Bunk 9 with five other girls: Jessica, Donnie, Fran, Karen, and Rory. My counselor is really nice. Her name is Patsy Kridell, and she's new this year too. She's from Texas, so she has a funny accent. All the girls imitate her. When we were getting organized, Patsy asked if anyone needed "he'p." Rory said, "The only one who needs he'p is you, Patsy. He'p talking right!" Everyone thought that was pretty funny.

Cousin Robin's next door in Bunk 10. That's where my best friend, Erin, is. I met her on the bus, and I was hoping we'd be in the same cabin, but it doesn't really matter because everyone's nice. I've made lots of friends already, and I'm having a great time.

It's really beautiful here. When you come to visit, I'll show you the lake. We went swimming this morning, and I saw tiny fish near the bottom, which isn't too deep where I'm allowed to swim since I haven't taken my swim test yet. But after I do, I think I'll be able to go all the way to the two floats, where the water must be pretty deep because there's a diving board on one of them. Anyhow, when you come to visit, we'll go swimming together.

But right now, rest hour's almost over, so I gotta scoot, scoot, skedaddle. I'll try to write again tomorrow. I miss you and love you so much!
Love,
Amy

The letter wasn't all lies: Camp *was* beautiful, the land having been tamed only where necessary for buildings, sports areas, and meeting places. I noticed the trees, their clean scent of pine, the moment we went through the gates. Girls belted out *We're here because we're here because we're here because we're here* as the bus rolled past the gatehouse and down a long pine-needled path to the recreation hall, where Uncle Ed and Pee-Wee Bassen, the athletic director, welcomed us with cabin assignments and lemonade. Uncle Ed winked at me when I lifted the icy pitcher. I shuddered, picturing how he always acted with my mother and remembering how he often reminded us that my father went to City College while he got to party and play ball at Penn State.

Aunt Helen hardly greeted him at the rec hall, but Robin made up for it, hugging her father as if it had been years since she'd seen him. "I promised my daughter here, Robin, a great summer," Uncle Ed said when he introduced himself. "And I know you'll all make that happen."

Pee-Wee led us to senior camp. With her squat body and slapdash haircut, she looked like someone who had always been chosen first for a sports team and last at a dance. "When you get to your cabins, ladies, start getting organized," she said. "No lollygagging now. And as soon as all the campers

31

are in, we'll ring the dinner bell. So let's go, Takawanda!" The girls took up the cheer:

Takawanda, Takawanda. We're the best.
Takawanda, Takawanda. Beats the rest.
Go, Takawanda!

We marched ahead. I looked for Erin. She walked with a group at the front of the pack while I straggled near the back.

I glanced around to get a sense of where I was. Athletic fields, tennis and basketball courts, blacktop areas for volleyball and badminton. I noticed a perfectly mowed spot with a flagpole in the middle. We passed what I later learned was junior camp, its clean white cabins clustered on two sides of a meadow. The path on which we walked grew wider as we approached the dining hall, built lakeside as if whoever designed Takawanda had started with that structure, choosing the best site for mealtimes.

I followed the girls along the water's edge, on a moist earthen trail sprinkled with pine cones. The path took us to senior camp, where six brown cabins with peeling green shutters sat in a clearing. Girls dropped arms from around each other's waists and raced for their summer homes.

I found Bunk 9, angled next to Bunk 10 as if these two cabins had been an afterthought, tacked up on the last spit of cleared land. Patsy held the door for me. "Well, let's see now." She dazzled me with her platinum blond hair. Not exactly my image of a camp counselor, this Marilyn Monroe look-alike with a thousand-watt smile. "You must be Amy. It's right nice to meet ya."

I set my bag on the only unclaimed bed, next to Donnie's, at the far end of the cabin, and looked around the room I had silenced with my entrance. Six beds in a row with the counselor's against the opposite wall; trunks all over the floor; and pine walls graffitied with reminders of past summers: LIZ WAS HERE, 1951. ALICE, 1957. BETTY AND CONNIE, FRIENDS FOREVER, '60. A construction paper job wheel, posted by the door, showed our names on an inner circle, our chores on an outer: bathroom; first sweep; second sweep; clothesline; trash; dining hall. While Rory was in the bathroom, Donnie told me that the names rotate each week, giving us at least one turn at every job. I found my name lined up with "dining hall."

"I'll make sure you meet the kitchen boys, Amy," Rory said at dinner that first night. We sat in the rear of the dining hall, Patsy at the head of our table with me to her left, next to Donnie.

"Yes indeed. The kitchen boys," Rory announced, clapping Jessica on the back. "But first, more cake!"

Everyone took seconds. Everyone but me.

If they serve sweets, don't eat too many. I heard my mother as if she had squeezed between Donnie and me. Hundreds of miles away, and her voice played in my head. I tried to shut her off.

"More cake!" Rory said again. "Enjoy it now, 'cause after tonight, seconds'll be hard to come by. Yes indeedy. Just 'cause Mr. Becker's real good-lookin' doesn't mean he won't be stingy to the bone like that last guy who ran this place."

"Rory!" Patsy's voice drew us to attention.

"What? It's true. The less he feeds us, the less it costs him. Simple as that. Or were you maybe jumping at the good-lookin' part, Patsy?"

"That's enough now. Mr. Becker's a right nice man, and I won't have you talkin' 'bout him that way. And he's family to Amy. So just watch what you say now. Ya hear?"

"Sure 'nough, Patsy. Anything to he'p Amy."

Giggles rose as if Rory had told a joke in a code only I couldn't break. Why did she keep poking fun at Patsy's accent? I loved my counselor's drawl and the way she tried to protect me.

The laughter continued until Donnie asked for thirds on dessert. Rory took the serving platter. She scraped her index finger in the extra icing and sucked off the chocolate.

"Yummy," she said, then slowly circled her tongue around her lips, ending her little show with kissing sounds. Snickers erupted again, full force.

"Don't you think that's funny, Amy?" Rory asked.

I studied my half-eaten piece of cake, my first and only piece. I didn't understand what was so funny, and I didn't know what I was supposed to say.

"Watch again," Rory instructed.

I looked at her, across the table, as she circled her tongue once more, then puckered her lips and kissed the air.

"Enough, Rory!" Patsy tried to stop her, but Rory revved up. Her tongue circled faster. More puckering. More kissing noises.

"Oh, yes!" Rory called out. "Practice for better things. Catch my drift, Amy?"

"That's all now!" Patsy said. "I mean it! I won't have any of that nonsense at my table or in my cabin. Ya hear?"

Rory rolled her eyes. "Aw, come on, Patsy. With a body like yours, why I'd guess you've had plenty of kissing practice—and more."

Jessica giggled. The rest of us stayed silent. Rory's words put worms in my stomach.

Patsy glared at Rory. "Just whatever are you fixin' to say?"

Rory didn't back down. "You know darn well what I'm *fixin' to say*."

Her mockery zipped a chill up my spine. I wondered how Rory had gotten so mean. Was intimidation a skill she had mastered, like playing the piano or swimming? "Practice makes perfect," my mother had said when I learned to swim my first summer at day camp. I shuddered at the thought that Rory might spend this summer practicing on me.

"Seems you've got boys on the brain, Rory," Patsy said. "But that's not what camp's about." Patsy pushed back from the table to get a cup of coffee from the "Counselors Only" urn on the side of the dining hall.

I tried to keep down the chocolate that rose in my throat.

"So, Amy Becker," Rory said, "I'll show you how we handle clean up around here since I do believe you're on dining hall duty this week." Rory chuckled as she motioned to the front of the room, where two metal pass-throughs in the pine-paneled wall opened into the kitchen. "See those two spaces?"

I nodded.

"Okay then. That place on the right's where the food comes out. Starting tomorrow, you'll have to bring it to the

table. Not like tonight, when everything was already here."
Rory dropped a chocolate-covered fork onto our tray and
pointed again to the front of the dining hall, showing off long
fingernails, painted a shimmery pink. Like cousin Robin—all
dolled up even at camp, as if appearance might buy happiness
here. As if big hair and nail polish were coins of friendship. As
if my mother were on to something with the way she always
put herself together. Was it only this morning she stood out in
her navy dress, so different from the other mothers?

"And that window on the left's where the dirty dishes go,"
Rory continued. "That's where the kitchen boys will be." She
grinned like the cat in *Alice in Wonderland*. "Are you listening
to me, Amy?"

"Come on, Rory," Donnie said as she stripped the last
smidgen of chocolate from her plate and put her dish on the
tray. "Ease up on her, okay?"

Rory ignored her. "Let's do it, Amy Becker. Follow me."

What would happen if I said no, that I was perfectly capa-
ble of bringing the tray up by myself? Would Rory get angry?
Would she be even meaner than she already was?

I picked up the tray and trailed Rory through the dining
hall. We passed Bunk 10's table, where Robin giggled with
the girls as if this were her fifth Takawanda summer. Past Erin,
who didn't look up, even when my elbow knocked her chair. I
followed Rory past other senior campers, who caught the song
my bunkmates started. Past the juniors, who meshed their
voices as if they were singing with one mouth:

> So high, I can't get over it.
> So low, I can't get under it.

So wide, I can't get around it.
Oh, rock-a my soul.

We walked past the sophomores and freshmen, heads drooping with fatigue. I followed Rory like a dutiful puppy.

She spoke again as we approached the owner's table, where Uncle Ed and Aunt Helen sat with Nancy and Pee-Wee and the camp nurse. "Now, Amy," Rory said, "make sure you introduce yourself to the kitchen boys. I'll see you back at our table after you've met them. Got it?"

I nodded.

"What's the matter? Cat got your tongue?"

"No," I answered, my voice barely audible.

Before she disappeared, Rory nudged me toward the line forming at the front of the dining hall: freshmen and sophomore counselors with leftovers and nearly clean dishes; junior campers in pairs, hauling plates and glasses splashed with bug juice ("Bug juice," Jessica had corrected me when I asked her to please pass the punch. "It's called bug juice. Not punch."); and seniors who scooted around me, eager to deposit their trays and escape the new girl they weren't supposed to talk to.

"Hey, little lady." The blackest face I had ever seen framed itself in the pass-through as I unloaded silverware. "I've been around long enough to spot a pretty new girl when I see one. Welcome to Takawanda."

I smiled at his velvety voice. "Thanks."

"The name's Clarence. Been running this kitchen since before you were born."

I started to introduce myself as a throat cleared behind me. I turned to face Erin, holding a pitcher. "Hey, Amy," she said with a smile.

"Hi!" My voice sounded as if it had been caged.

"I knew Rory'd make you do this. God, I hate her."

"Let's go, ladies." Pee-Wee bussed leftovers from the owner's table. "No lollygagging now."

"Just a sec," Erin said, then whispered to me, "I think I know what Rory's up to, and it could be even worse if the boys think you're flirting with them. So just tell Rory you met them, the kitchen boys: Andy and Jed."

"Andy and Jed?"

"Right." Erin's pitcher clanked the metal pass-through. "I gotta go before Rory sees me."

I repeated the names to myself: *Andy and Jed. Andy and Jed.* What did Erin mean about flirting with them and making things worse? Something to do with my initiation? And that's when I knew what Rory had done: She had turned the job wheel to stick me with dining hall duty.

She started in as soon as I returned to our table. "You met them, right? The kitchen boys?"

Her question sent a tingle up my back. I eked out a measly "Uh-huh."

"What'd you say?"

"Rory!" Patsy squared her shoulders. "I don't like your tone of voice. We're family for the summer, and I expect us to act like one."

Rory looked from Patsy to me. "Why that's exactly what I'm doing, Patsy. Treating old Amy here like family. Isn't that right, girls?"

"Now you heard what I said, Rory, and I mean it. I don't appreciate that tone, and I'll bet your mama and daddy'd be real disappointed to hear you talk like that."

"Well, it's a good thing we're not betting then. 'Cause you don't know squat about my family. Why, my *mama* and *daddy*'d feel right at home with this kind of talk."

Nancy ended their battle when she stood in the front of the dining hall to lead the Takawanda welcome:

We welcome you to summer camp.
We're mighty glad you're here.
We'll send the air reverberating
With a mighty cheer.
We'll sing you in. We'll sing you out.
To you we'll raise a mighty shout.
Hail, hail, the gang's all here,
And you're welcome to our great camp.

Even Rory sang out. She looked right at me while I prayed she would drown in the lake.

Chapter 4

Please Don't Let Them Hurt Me

I forced myself to smile the next day at lunch when Rory asked, "What did the elephant say to the naked man?" She answered her own riddle: "How do you eat with that thing?" I laughed even though I didn't get it then. I laughed even when Patsy said, "Now stop it, all of you. I thought we had an understanding, Rory. No more of that talk, and I don't care if your mama and daddy'd think it's okay. It's not, and I won't have it at this table or in our cabin. Is that clear?"

"Why perfectly, ma'am," Rory answered, like a lady who had never heard a dirty joke.

•

"Let's go!" Rory ordered during our first rest hour. She spoke from the foot of Donnie's bed, not ten minutes into our letter-writing session. "Meeting with Bunk 10. Nature hut. Remember?"

"Give us a break," Donnie answered, sitting cross-legged on her Hudson Bay blanket, the blanket all my bunkmates had, the only item on the camp list—other than new sneakers—my mother had refused to buy. Why spend money for a fancy blanket with stripes when we could buy a plain green one on sale? "Ease up, Rory," Donnie kept on. "I'm writing to my folks."

"Not anymore you're not." Rory ripped the paper off Donnie's pad.

"Give it back. Come on. I want to get this letter done."

"Well, la-de-da. Like it matters what you say to your parents. Like they'll really read your dumb letter."

Donnie stood up. "Look, I'm sorry if you have trouble with your folks, Rory, but—"

"Shut up! Don't you dare say that again." Rory balled up Donnie's letter and took a long shot toward the trash can at the front of the cabin.

Donnie crawled back onto her bed. She opened her writing pad and chewed on her pen.

I peeked at Rory, holding her ground at the foot of Donnie's bed, stretching her arms and studying her shiny pink nails as she spoke. "If you're thinking of starting another letter, don't bother. We haven't got time for that nonsense."

"But we need meal tickets," Jessica piped up.

Rory strolled toward her own bed, next to Jessica's. She flicked Fran and Karen on their legs as she passed. "Patsy won't know to check our mail, her being new and all. And we're certainly not gonna waste senior rest hour privileges sitting in the cabin waiting for our counselor to keep us in line. So just stuff a blank sheet in an envelope and address it home. It's meeting time, girls. Jess, Fran, Karen, Donnie, let's go!"

I kept writing, pretending not to listen. Meeting time for everyone but me. Time to plan my initiation, no doubt.

The screen door creaked when Rory opened it, then slapped shut behind the girls as they dropped blank pages onto Patsy's bed and went out. Donnie was the last to leave. At the door, she glanced back and shrugged her shoulders.

Would Robin meet with them? Would Erin? Alone in the cabin, I looked through the screen, where a window pane should have been, out at the senior camp tetherball, at bathing suits slung over clotheslines, at the door to Erin's cabin. Loneliness clumped in my chest.

Patsy breezed in while I was still working on my letter to Charlie. "Well, hey there, Amy," she said just as I wrote about the great time I was having with all my new friends. "What're you doin' all alone in here, gal?"

I wanted to tell Patsy about Rory and the meal tickets. About the meeting in the nature hut, that the girls were planning to do something awful to me. I wanted to tell Patsy I was sorry I had laughed at lunch, that I didn't even understand Rory's riddle. Yet before I could say anything, the knot in my chest loosened, releasing tears.

I let Patsy hold me the way I imagined a mother would comfort a child who had gotten picked on at recess. I took a long breath, filling my nose with the smell of Noxema. It hung in the air from the night before, when Rory and Jessica had coated their faces with cream and reminded us that "our first social, with the Saginaw boys, will be here before you know it."

Patsy hugged me tight. "I don't know what in tarnation those gals have done," she said, her accent as embracing as her arms, "but I want you to know that I, for one, am right glad you're here."

I had to tell her about the initiation. This would be the time—maybe the only time—to ask her to protect me. I sighed as Patsy eased her grip. She held me at arm's length.

"Thanks, Patsy. I'm...well, I'm glad *you're* here too. And there's something—"

"Now I know what you're fixin' to say, about laughing at the lunch table."

"But—"

"No need to explain, gal." Patsy dropped her hands, though she continued to hold me with her deep blue eyes. "I know what it's like tryin' to fit in, 'specially when everyone else knows one another. Why, I've got just that same problem with the staff. The way they criticize your Uncle Ed, it's downright sinful, always comparing the way he wants things done with how the former owner did things. And I can't really say anything without alienatin' myself. But I'll tell you this: Your uncle seems to be a mighty fine man. And he sure is handsome. That's one thing the staff agrees on." Patsy grinned. "A regular James Dean kinda guy, I'd say. But I can't speak up and tell the other counselors to mind their p's and q's. No siree. So sometimes I pretend to go along with what they say, like what you did at lunch, laughin' with Rory and the others. But don't you worry 'bout that, 'cause I know you didn't mean any harm. You're a fine gal, real well-mannered. I saw that right away, that your parents have done a right good job raisin' you."

Patsy pulled a tissue from the box on my cubby and handed it to me. "So remember, Amy, we're in this together. We're both here to have a good summer. That's what I'm fixin' to do. And that's what I want for you as well."

I wiped my face and smiled. So what if Patsy thought Uncle Ed was handsome, sexy even? That had nothing to do with me.

My counselor hugged me hard again. And when she did, the screen door groaned. I slipped out of Patsy's arms as Rory walked in, my bunkmates in tow.

●

"Amy, you lied to us." Rory addressed me from her bed after lights out.

"What do you mean?" Fear choked my words.

"You lied to us, and people who lie get punished. Isn't that right, girls?"

A flashlight beamed through the screen door, aiming like a rifle at each bed. "Bunk 9, pipe down in there." The on-duty counselor used a schoolteacher voice. "And if I have to warn you ladies again, I'll spend this OD shift sitting *in* your cabin."

Silence filled the room while the light scanned us again. Then the creak of the wooden stoop, the counselor settling in by our door. *Please stay*, I prayed. *Please don't go away.*

I lay frozen with fright. How had I lied? And what would they do to me?

The cabin stilled, the eye of the hurricane. Not a ruffling of blankets and sheets. Not a sneeze or a throat-clearing. No, this wouldn't be a prank like my bra up the flagpole. Rory's accusation, the way she had stretched *lied* into two syllables, signaled something darker.

I wished I had confided in Patsy. Now all my hope rested with the counselor by our door. *Please don't go away*, I prayed again.

But the stoop creaked. Then soft footsteps. The crunching of pine needles and twigs.

"Shhh." The warning came from the front of the cabin. It had to be Rory. My heart galloped in my ears. "She's going to the counselor shack." Yes, Rory's voice. I knew it even in a whisper. "That bridge game in there'll go on for hours. But we'll wait a few minutes just to be safe, make sure she's gone for good."

This was it then. My initiation. Oh my God.

"So you lied to us, Amy," Rory said again.

"About what?" was all I could think to say. Tears burned the back of my eyes. *Don't let them hear you cry*, I warned myself.

"You said you met the kitchen boys, Andy and Jed. But I talked to them, and I know you didn't. So you just stay where you are while we get ready for your special introduction. You got that?"

I tried to slip into my mother's armor: no outer world in; no inner world out. But my tears wouldn't stop.

"I said you got that, Amy Becker?" Rory asked once more.

"Enough, Rory," Donnie whispered. "And in case you forgot, she's the owner's niece. This could really get you in trouble."

I wanted to reach out to her, my new friend. But fear kept me still, my blanket pulled tight around me. When would Patsy get back from her night out? She had told us she was heading into town with the other first-year counselors. Uncle Ed had offered to drive them, she had said.

"You think I'm that stupid, Donnie-girl?" Rory's voice stayed hushed. "Well, we don't have to worry about Mr. Becker. Robin, his daughter, is coming with us. Everyone is. And Amy won't snitch to anyone. Isn't that right, Amy Becker? It's been two days, and I know you by now."

Rory didn't wait for my answer. "So Donnie-girl," she continued, "you're either with *us* or with *her*. And if you're with her, you get the same treatment she does. Your choice."

"Okay. Okay," Donnie whispered. "Let's just do it already."

"Don't be so hasty. The boys aren't meeting us till ten-thirty, and the counselors off duty won't be back till midnight. So let's take our time and do this the right way."

On Rory's command, the girls got out of bed and found their flashlights.

"Good. I think we're set." Rory's tone softened, even in a whisper. "Now there's nothing to be scared of, Amy. Just a little something we planned, a special way for you to meet those kitchen boys you lied about."

I focused on Rory's words, trying to ignore the turning in my stomach. *Please, God,* I prayed. *Please don't let them hurt me.*

"So get up and out of your nightgown," Rory ordered. "And don't bother getting dressed. You won't need any clothes."

Someone giggled.

"Knock it off," Rory said, then addressed me once more. "Just put your robe on, and take your flashlight...no...on second thought, no flashlight. You won't need that either."

I wriggled from my blanket and stood in the cool air. Why couldn't I say no? *No, Rory. I'm not coming.* I tried to push the words from my mouth, but nothing came. Without a sound, I stripped off my nightgown, reached for my robe—on the nail with my laundry bag—and shivered as I put it on.

"Blindfold her," Rory whispered.

Jessica used what felt like the tie from a starched beach robe, the terry cloth scratchy on my face. "And make sure it's tight enough so she can't see anything." Jessica yanked the band until I thought my heart would shoot through my skull.

"Now, Donnie, since you've been telling me to ease up, I'm putting you in charge of leading her with me. And don't even think of doing anything stupid." With Rory pulling me by my left arm and Donnie guiding me by my right, we stepped into the night. I heard Jessica, Fran, and Karen behind us.

"Shhh," Rory commanded, when we met another group, the girls from Bunk 10, I assumed. "No talking. You all know the plan."

A path. Definitely, we were on a path, stamping twigs and pine cones. Then the sound of water, the cry of a loon. Its scream echoed my fear. Donnie jumped. "Jesus H. Christ," Rory said. "It's just a stupid loon. And watch where you aim that flashlight."

We marched in silence after that, the trail to the lake longer in darkness. Roots spiked up, jabbing my toes. I wondered where Erin was. She couldn't be part of this plot. And Robin? Where was my cousin in all this?

The path smoothed over. Fewer twigs. Fewer bumps. Then sand. The lakefront. *Please, God. Please don't let them hurt me.*

"Okay, girls. Flashlights off."

Still blindfolded, I felt them gather around.

"Ever go skinny-dipping, Amy?" Rory wanted to know.

Panic smothered my voice.

"I said, ever go skinny-dipping?"

I couldn't answer.

"Okay. Doesn't matter. You're about to go now. But first, anyone want a look before she meets the boys?"

"No way, Rory. That's not what we said." Was that Erin, all hushed and shaky?

"Just the swimming part." I recognized Donnie, even in whispers. "Nothing else."

"Listen, you. This is the last time I'll say it: You're either with *us* or with *her*. Now which'll it be?"

"But that's not what we talked about." Erin again. This time I was sure.

"Drop the robe, Amy," Rory ordered. "And keep that blindfold on. Nothing for you to see yet. We'll do all the looking, if you catch my drift."

"Cut it out, Rory. It's not funny anymore." A voice I hadn't heard much: Fran or Karen trying to rescue me.

"Oh, you want funny? I'll give you funny all right." Rory's tone slapped me. "Donnie, Erin, Karen, if you give me any more trouble, you're going in with her. How's that? Funny enough?"

"How's this, Rory? We're all going in with her." A new speaker, followed by a buzz of muted chatter. I didn't know who said what, but it didn't matter. Whatever they planned for me, however awful it might be, I wouldn't be alone.

Someone freed me from the blindfold. I clutched my robe and blinked into the hazy crowd, visible by moonlight and the beam of Rory's flashlight. Everyone in nightgowns, sweatshirts over them. "All right, girls," Rory said. "You win. The kitchen boys aren't here yet. So you want a little skinny-dip? Go right ahead. But be fast about it, 'cause once the boys get here, we're back to our plan. And if you're still in when they arrive, you'll just have to find a way to your clothes while I hold the light."

Nobody moved. Having tested their power against Rory's, they knew they had lost. The boys were coming. How could they go skinny-dipping?

So there I was: alone again.

"Okay now," Rory said. "If anyone's thinking of doing anything stupid like trying to leave or calling for a counselor—anything stupid like that—just forget it. 'Cause what happens to Amy tonight will be nothing compared to what'll happen to anyone who's not with me. So drop the robe, Amy. It's time for a swim."

I pulled my robe tighter. "Um, I'm not really a good swimmer." The lie rolled off my tongue. If I could convince Rory I couldn't swim, she probably wouldn't throw me in, wouldn't take a chance on my drowning. Even Rory couldn't be that cruel, right?

"You see, girls," Rory said. "Another lie. First she tells us she met Andy and Jed. Then she tells us she doesn't swim. But

I know she took her swim test this morning. Passed with flying colors, I hear." Rory's flashlight pierced my robe. I trembled as I felt her picturing my body, imagining her gift to the boys. "Guess you thought I didn't know about those ten laps you did between the floats. But see, you've learned something already, Amy Becker: I find out everything that goes on around here. So off with the robe now. We'd like to see those laps. Wouldn't we, girls?"

That's when I heard them, their footsteps packing the sand. Rory shined her light on the feet of two approaching boys. "Guess you won't be meeting them in the water, after all. Shhh," she warned, as the boys drew closer. Rory wove her rays up their legs, then rested her beam on their bathing trunks. "Howdy, fellas," she crooned, her whispery voice coated with honey. "Here's the surprise I promised you." She bathed my body in light. "Her name's Amy, and she's all yours. Ready for a little strip action?"

Now I knew why Erin had stopped me from meeting them. She didn't want the boys to think I was looking for trouble. And more than that, my shame would be less if I didn't know the ones who would stare, the kitchen boys who would take me in, naked breasts and all.

I tried to breathe, but the air stuck in my throat. *Don't cry*, I told myself again. Then shallow breaths. In. Out. In. Out. No outer world in; no inner world out. Like mother, like daughter. *Don't cry. Don't feel.*

"I'm not gonna say it another time." Rory's voice became itself again, pointed and sharp. "Drop the robe."

"Please don't make me do this."

"I'll make you do anything I damn well please. Am I right, girls, or am I right?"

"Right again, Rory," Jessica agreed.

"Now I promised the boys here a little something special, and I'm not going back on my word. I'm not a liar like you." Rory's light hit my eyes. "So either you take that robe off right now, or we'll help you do it."

"Please, no." My voice came like a five-year-old's.

"Erin. Donnie. I'm giving you the honors then. Get that robe off her...unless...unless you boys want to do it."

The boys came in close.

No. Please, God. Please don't let them do this.

"Ummm, Rory...we need to talk." It was one of the boys, close enough to me now to slide the robe off my shoulders. "You said it'd be a swim. A coed swim. Some wicked good fun. That's all."

"And we c-c-can't do anything like th-th-this." A boy who stutters—probably picked on his whole life—wouldn't hurt me, I wanted to believe.

The first boy spoke again. "What Jed means is we can't do anything that gets us in trouble. We can't afford to lose our jobs."

"So what are you, Andy?" Rory asked. "Chicken or pussy?"

Jessica laughed. "Chicken or pussy. That's good, Rory."

"Shut up, Jess."

"Sorry," Andy said. "We'll stay for a swim. But that's all."

"Okay. Okay. I'll give the girls the honors then. You boys just watch. No harm in that, right? Erin, Donnie, take her robe."

"No. I'm leaving," Erin answered.

"No you're not. Remember what I told you? If you're not with me, what happens to you will be worse."

"I'm going," Erin said. "And you don't have to listen to her either, Amy." Erin stepped away from the group.

"Wait up," Donnie said. "I'm coming with you."

"Anyone else want to join them?" Rory asked. "'Cause here's your chance. But I'll tell you this: You cross me now, I'll cross you later. And when I do, you'll find out what a dumb choice you made."

"Wait," Fran said. "I'm coming."

"Me too."

"Me too."

Five girls left. Six stayed, including Robin. The line was drawn. The war had officially begun.

Chapter 5

A Little Fun with the New Girl

"So, fellas," Rory said, counting Andy and Jed in her ranks, "ready for that swim now?"

"Nah. Some other time. It's getting late."

"Right. We g-g-gotta go."

"Not so fast. It won't kill you to have some fun, you know, seeing as last summer you said Clarence practically works you to death in that kitchen. So how 'bout it? You don't have to strip her. Just take her for a swim. Hell, she says she's not that strong, could probably use a little help coming in from the floats—especially if that big old snapping turtle bites her feet, say, or her boobs."

Jessica led a round of giggles and arm slapping.

"Quiet." Rory wasn't looking for levity. "So whaddaya say, boys? I'm giving you a chance to be heroes."

Don't just stand here. Move! I ordered myself. *Do something. Scream.* But my feet stayed glued to the sand, and my voice deserted me, like the girls who had disappeared in the name of support.

Andy turned from the group that closed in on me again. "Let's go, Jed."

"Hold it, you two," Rory said. "You're worried about losing your jobs? Well, go ahead and leave then. Ruin our little initiation and see how fast they boot you outta here."

"Wh-whaddaya mean?"

"Come on," Andy said. "We're going."

"No, w-w-wait. Wh-whaddaya saying, Rory?"

"It's simple. You leave, I'll tell everyone you raped our new friend. Raped her right here on the beach and made us all watch. See how long you'll keep your jobs when Mr. Becker hears that."

"That's enough." Andy again. "Come on, Jed."

"B-b-but—"

"Don't worry." Andy pulled Jed's arm. "When we tell Mr. Becker what really happened, we won't be the ones in trouble."

"Jesus H. Christ. Even *you* can't be that stupid, Andy." Rory's light found Andy's face. "Who the hell do you think he'll believe: two local-yokels, one who can't even talk worth a damn, or campers whose parents pay big bucks to send them here? You leave now, and we'll see who gets in trouble when we tell Mr. Becker what you boys did to poor, little Amy, especially when he hears it from his very own daughter." Rory spotlighted my cousin. "Right, Robin?"

Say no, Robin. I tried to loosen the words, which caught in my throat. *Tell her you won't lie. Tell her to let me go, Robin.*

My cousin studied the sand. Why wasn't she helping me? Sure, we were as different from each other as our parents were. But still, we were family. How could she not try to save me?

"Okay." Rory's voice stayed hushed. "Let's start again. You pot-scrubbing twerps get your sneakers off. You're going in. And you, Amy Becker, drop the robe. We're running out of time."

I clutched my robe tight and looked at Rory's gang, heads down. None but Rory and Jessica watched as Rory's light played on my body. "Do it, Jess."

Jessica tugged at the robe.

"No. Stop!" Andy called out.

"Shut up or you've already washed your last dish," Rory said, forgetting to whisper. "It's showtime. Get that robe off her, Jess."

"Let's go, Jed."

"Maybe he wants to stay," Rory said. "Maybe I've had it all wrong. Maybe *he's* the smart one."

"I'm leaving." Andy started off slowly, inviting Jed to follow.

Rory offered a different invitation. "Wanna undress her, Jed? Have a little fun with the new girl? A wicked good time?"

Jed watched Andy go, then tracked the beam from Rory's light to my robe. Time froze while Jed considered.

Run! Now! I told myself, but my legs didn't listen.

"No. Andy's r-r-right. B-bye."

"All right, girls. Glad none of you are as stupid as they are, walking away when the fun's about to start."

Rory and Jessica ripped off my robe and tossed it toward the lake. I crossed my arms over my chest.

Rory's flashlight settled on my underpants. "Well, lookie here. Amy's got panties on. Now how can she go skinny-dipping if she's not naked?" The light arced from my underwear to my crossed arms and back down. "Get 'em off, girl."

My throat closed. I choked as I hugged my shoulders.

"Oh, let her swim like that," a camper from Bunk 10 piped up. "She's embarrassed enough."

"You shut up or you're going in too."

"Come on, Rory," another girl said. "Just throw her in with her panties on. What's the big deal?"

"Jesus! You cowards should've gone with Erin's group. Would've given me more to look forward to when I punish those chickens."

I squeezed my knees together.

"Take 'em off, Amy. I'm tired of playing with you."

"No!" My cry forced itself out.

"Shut up. Someone'll hear you."

Finally I found my legs. I kicked off my flip-flops and ran, arms still crossed on my chest.

"Grab her," Rory ordered.

They wrestled me to the sand.

"One more move and you're dead, Amy Becker." Rory's fingernails scraped my skin when she yanked down my panties.

"No!" I lowered my arms, tried to hide my crotch from Rory's light.

"Cover her trap, Jess. And keep it covered." Rory hurled my underwear toward the lake. "The rest of you, pick her up."

Only Jessica moved, slamming a hand over my mouth. The back of my head dug into the sand.

"Let's go. I told you to pick her up. Now!"

They pulled me to my feet, unclenching my arms. My tears flowed as Rory's flashlight played peekaboo with my breasts, my groin. I squeezed my knees tighter. *Don't cry. Don't feel.*

"Time for that swim," Rory said. "At last. So two on her arms and two on her legs. Robin, you're legs."

Robin and one of her bunkmates grabbed my ankles and lifted me while Rory's light fixed on my crotch. "Want a good look at your cousin?" Rory asked as she slithered between the girls at my feet, inching Robin over.

No answer.

"Come on, Robin." Rory kept her light on me as they carried me toward the lake. "Didn't you and Amy ever play doctor, you being family and all. So how 'bout a little game now?"

"No." Robin's voice was a whisper. "I'm . . . I'm not into girls."

"Well then. We'll just see what action you whip up with the Saginaw boys."

They hauled me to the end of the dock. The cold air pressed my body as they lay me on my back. Wooden planks rammed my spine. My nipples stood like pencil erasers. I tried to roll onto my stomach, to escape into water.

"Don't even think of it," Rory said, setting her flashlight down and grabbing my ankles. "You'll go in when I say so."

I folded my arms across my chest again, squeezed my knees as hard as I could.

"Okay. Now. Do it, Jess," Rory said, freeing my legs.

Jessica's hands were clammy on my shoulders. I hit the water before she could shove me, let the lake take me alive.

Chapter 6

I'd Rather Eat Worms

I threw up on the sand, then crept toward senior camp, shivering as I went. Rory had made off with my robe, no doubt, when she and her gang scrambled back to bed, leaving me alone in the lake. No clothing. No light. Just my flip-flops, where I'd finally kicked them off to run.

I stumbled into the black cabin, arms shielding my crotch, my breasts, in case Rory played with her flashlight. But there wasn't any light. No light and no sound. Only a stifled giggle from Jessica. Yet I knew Rory wasn't finished with me.

I sneaked into bed, the blanket soggy from my robe. Rory had put it there, I imagined. It dripped reminders: I didn't belong here; the girls didn't like me; I wouldn't survive. What would they do to me next?

I shook from the cold and the damp. From embarrassment. Disgrace. Oh my God, they'd seen me naked. I curled into a ball. *Don't cry*, I warned myself again. But I couldn't blink back tears.

I felt the hand as if in a dream. Was that Donnie, reaching out from the bed next to mine? She passed me my nightgown. I snuggled into it as exhaustion rolled through me. Yet sleep didn't come. I closed my eyes, and there was my mother. *It's your fault, Amy. Robin's new too and they didn't throw her in, did they?* If I hadn't worn the uniform to the bus, I thought, if Charlie hadn't made a scene, we wouldn't be at war. If I were sexy like my cousin, Rory might have spared me. If I had big hair and polished nails, the girls might have liked me. Yes, my mother was right: I was responsible. It was my fault for not having a good body. My fault for not understanding dirty jokes. My fault for not being popular. Why would anyone want to be my friend? I cried myself to sleep—silent tears so no one would notice.

●

In the morning, I avoided Rory's eyes and ignored her stupid grin. Patsy said I looked like "a frightened jackrabbit ready to run."

"Bad dreams, I guess," I told her, wishing more than anything that were true. And when Donnie and Erin asked if I was okay, I used my mother's end-of-discussion tone: "I'm fine. I just don't want to talk about it."

Only Nancy wouldn't let me get away with that. After lunch, she summoned Erin and me to the head counselor's cabin. It was nestled by the lake on the fringe of junior camp, as silent at rest hour as the waterfront the night before.

All morning the scene had played in my mind: Rory's hands on my underpants; her light on my crotch; the dock; the water. Dark. Cold. All morning I had prayed Rory would die. I wanted it to happen in the lake, Rory flailing her arms and screaming for help, a snapping turtle zooming in between her legs.

Now Erin and I draped our legs over Nancy's bed and pumped our feet to the rhythm of the lake. "I'd rather eat worms than listen to Rory all summer," Erin said.

Nancy, in the middle, put her arms around our shoulders. "Clarence said the boys told him it got nasty. I'm so sorry, Amy." Nancy massaged my back. I welcomed her touch, the warmth of her words. "But why didn't you tell me? Why didn't you come to me without my calling for you?"

My throat closed, blocking words.

"I swear," Erin chimed in, "I'm not gonna let Rory boss us around anymore the way she does every summer. God, it just makes me so angry, how she treated Amy. Even worse than what she did to me two years ago. And I really thought if I went back to the cabin, if enough of the girls followed me, then Rory would give up and leave Amy alone. But no, not Rory. Always needs to show how powerful she is. And never you mind who gets hurt."

"What did she do to you, Amy?" Nancy's fingers pressed into my shoulders. "I need to know exactly what she did."

"Tell her, Amy," Erin pleaded. "You have to."

The water. The lake that had swallowed me. My embarrassment was too great; my fear, too heavy. "If you tell, you're dead," Rory had warned when she heard Nancy call for me.

"Remember," Rory whispered as we left the dining hall, checking to see that Patsy lagged behind, "if you ever tell anyone, you'll be really sorry. And anyhow, it was just a skinny-dip, just a little fun. In fact, you enjoyed it. Didn't you, Amy Becker?"

"Please, Amy." Nancy pushed harder. "You need to tell me what happened."

I swallowed hard. *Don't talk. Don't feel.*

"I have to know what they did," Nancy tried again.

"I'm sorry," I answered, invoking my mother's tone. "I can't talk about it."

"Not talking won't make it go away, Amy," Nancy said. "Not talking won't make it all right. You have to tell me."

I couldn't look at her. Instead, I took in Nancy's cabin, a miniature Bunk 9, save the shades at the windows, real windows. And a fan, propped on a wooden table in the corner. A sink on one wall, mirrored medicine cabinet over it. A weathered dresser with clipboards on top. No living out of a trunk like a camper. I longed to haul over my sleeping bag and move into the head counselor's cabin for the rest of the season. No more threats. No more Rory.

"I'm all right," I lied. "I just don't want to talk about it. I just want to go home."

Erin reached across Nancy to pat my knee. "You can't go home. I mean, even if you could, you can't. 'Cause then Rory wins, don't you see? 'Cause then she believes she has power over everyone.

"And you can't go home 'cause you're my friend. I knew it as soon as I saw you at the bus, when I saw you with your brother." Erin kicked her sneakers to the floor and pulled her legs up onto Nancy's blue blanket. "So you can't go home," she went on, angling herself toward Nancy and me, "'cause you're gonna be my best camp friend."

I breathed in, long and deep, filling myself with the promise of friendship.

"See, Nance," Erin said. "Not to worry. I'll take care of her."

"Good. You can start by telling me what happened last night."

"I left before they did anything," Erin answered. "Honest. I didn't see it." She glanced down for a moment, then turned toward me again. Tears filled her eyes, which darted around Nancy's cabin as she spoke. "I'm really sorry, Amy. I should have pulled you away with me," Erin explained. "But I was scared Rory would come after us and hurt you even more. The only reason I went to the stupid lake in the first place was I thought I'd be able to help you there. But Rory had it all planned. We couldn't stop her. Honest, I tried. And she said if I warned you or told anyone, she'd get both of us. And she said she'd make it even worse if she thought anyone knew. And I really wanted to tell you, but I knew she'd find out. Somehow she'd know. So I couldn't say anything." Erin slowed for a breath. "I'm really, really sorry." She let her eyes find mine as Nancy stood.

Erin and I got up as well. Erin hugged me, and the only thing I could do was cry.

"So you're still not going to tell me what happened?" Nancy asked.

Now that I allowed myself to feel, I wanted Nancy to know what Rory had done. I wanted Rory kicked out of camp. But then Rory would know I had told. And she'd find a way to get me before she'd start packing. "I'm okay," I said once more.

Nancy's arms drifted back to our shoulders. "I'll let you go in two shakes. But about last night…well, I suppose I can't force you to talk about it. So I just want you to hear this: I'm always available to both of you. You come and visit anytime. And I'll make sure the staff keeps an eye on Rory."

"Thanks, Nance." Erin slipped from Nancy's arm, then hugged her while I stood there, wanting to.

Dear Charlie,

I'm having a great time at camp. The girls are super nice, and we all get along really well.

We went swimming at night. Yes, at night! The campers who've been here before said they have a special night swim at the start of each summer. It's sort of a tradition, a way to welcome new campers. The water was freezing, but it was fun jumping in, in the dark. Some of the girls tried to scare me by talking about a snapping turtle, but Erin, my best friend, said they just made that up—kind of a joke they play on new campers.

We're finally settled in, and all the activities are starting. I signed up for intensive tennis, a double period for girls who already know how to play.

Well, I gotta scoot, scoot, skedaddle. I miss you, buddy, and I love you so much.

Love,
Amy

P.S. Tell Mom and Dad to write me about what you've been doing—and tell them please not to mention the night swim to Uncle Ed. It's a secret, and I don't want anyone to get in trouble.

●

I was as surprised to see cousin Robin at the tennis courts as she seemed to see me. With all her complaining about tennis lessons in the winter, I expected her to sign up for other activities with Rory's gang—nature or drama, perhaps, where you wouldn't sweat or mess your hair. Arts and crafts maybe, where I heard you could make earrings and pins using tweezers to pick up tiny enamel bits, guaranteed not to chip your nail polish.

Jody sent the juniors to the hard courts with two counselors, then huddled with the seniors by the three red clay ones. "We're just gonna do a little warm-up hitting today," she said as she scanned our group. "See how you all play."

Robin and I, assigned to the same court, walked silently next to each other. *How could you, Robin?* I wanted to scream. My cousin turned toward me for a second, as if I had asked the question aloud. I felt like my clothes were invisible, leaving me as naked as I'd been the night before.

Jody reached into a shopping cart brimming with tennis balls. She tossed five or six our way. Two girls from Bunk 8 sprinted to the other side of the net.

Robin bounced a ball as if it were a Spalding. *A my name is Alice, and my husband's name is Al.* A few years earlier, we were giggling together, turning our legs up and over on the bounce. How could Robin have sided with Rory?

My cousin took her time as if sorting through thoughts. Ready to apologize maybe?

"Come on. Let's start!" our opponents yelled.

Robin hooked me with her eyes. "How 'bout we forget this hitting nonsense and play a game?" she said.

"But Jody told us just to hit," I answered. *Say it, Robin. Say you're sorry.*

"Little Miss Perfect, always does what she's told," Robin said instead. "Goody-two-shoes Amy. And then my father wants to know why *I'm* not helpful, why *I* don't make honor roll. Well, at least I have friends. At least I'm popular. And I sure would have yelled and fought harder at the lake."

How could Robin think the initiation had been my fault? That's one thing my cousin and my mother would agree on: They'd say I was to blame.

"Come on!" the Bunk 8 girls hollered. "Hit the ball already!"

"What's the rush?" Robin asked. "We've got two full periods."

"Let's just hit," I said.

"Why? 'Cause that's what the counselor said?" Robin's stare gave me goose bumps. "Well, I for one don't care what Jody says," she went on. "We're gonna play this game right, show those Bunk 8 campers who rules." Robin watched me hug the baseline. "So get ready."

"I am."

"No you're not. You need to be up by the net."

"Why?"

"'Cause that's where you're supposed to stand when your partner serves. Jesus, Amy, if you don't even know that, you don't belong in intensive."

I felt as if my cousin had rammed the ball down my throat as I inched toward the service line. I had played only singles. How far up was I supposed to go? *Say you're sorry, Robin. Say you're sorry.* The words repeated in my head.

I turned to see Robin holding the ball in the air, signaling our opponents. "I don't need a warm-up. These are good."

Ever play doctor with your cousin? Rory's question rattled in my brain.

Hit the ball, Amy. Smack it hard. It's Rory's face, I imagined. Her perfect hair, her made-up eyes.

"Wow! Good shot!" one of the girls called when I slammed a forehand. "Where'd you learn to hit like that?"

"Good question," Robin said.

"My father taught me."

"Uncle Lou? Well, go figure." Robin studied the ball for a moment. "Just another Becker secret, I guess: your father teaching you tennis. And all this time I thought it was Aunt Sonia who had all the secrets."

"What do you mean?"

"Come on. You know damn well what I mean. All those things about your mother we're not allowed to talk about."

What did Robin know about my mother? What things? What secrets?

Hit the ball, Amy. Smack it hard. It's Robin now. Her hair rollers and four-poster bed. Her record player, which my mother said I didn't need for the pop music I listened to on the radio. A record player would be too expensive.

Hit the ball, Amy. It's Robin's precious records, her Everly Brothers collection spilling from her bookcase without any books. *Wake up, little Susie. Wake up!* What secrets, I wondered again. What did my cousin know that I didn't?

Jody stood by the court. "What's going on here, ladies? I thought I told you just to hit."

"Sorry, Jody," Robin singsonged. "We thought you said we could play."

"Eager beavers, huh? Well, go ahead then. Keep playing. I'll just watch for a while. See how you do."

A Bunk 8 camper readied her serve. "New game. The score's one-love."

"That's love-one," Robin said. "Server's score first."

Cousin Robin sounded like Rory. She grabbed the power. She needed to win. She said she knew secrets. Secrets about my mother. I wanted to ask again what she was talking about. But I couldn't let on that she knew more than I did.

I felt Jody's eyes on me, waiting for my return. *Hit the ball, Amy.*

"Great shot, kiddo." Jody applauded. "No wonder you wanted to play."

"Beginner's luck," Robin mumbled.

"Everyone take a water break," Jody called across the courts. "It's hotter than blazes. A regular heat wave."

Robin raced for the fountain. I propped my racket against the net, then walked toward the line of girls eager for drinks. Jody came up beside me. "You're a natural, kiddo. I'm glad you're in intensive. And don't forget to put your name up on the board for the senior round-robin tournament."

●

"So, gals, how did activities go?" Patsy tried to energize us in the thick evening heat that blanketed the dining hall. "Come on, y'all. No answers from my chatterboxes? Nobody willin' to tell me 'bout their day?"

Rory broke the silence. "Oh, like you really give a damn about our dumb activities."

"Rory!" Campers turned to stare as Patsy's voice flew through the room. I caught Erin's eyes and exchanged a quick smile.

"What? You think you can fool us? Asking about our day as if you really care."

"See, you're wrong 'bout that." Patsy spoke softly now.

"Yeah, right. What do you think we are? Stupid? I know all you care about: a nice big man. Yes indeedy. Catch my drift, girls?"

"Enough!" Patsy tried to stop her, while Jessica banged a spoon on the table. The rest of us sipped bug juice and moved food around our plates.

"Well, it's the truth," Rory kept on. "And it's Mr. Becker you want. I see how you look at him, how he looks at you. I know what you two are fixin' to do."

Patsy seemed to ignore the comment. "Amy," she said, turning toward me, finding her gentlest voice, "would you go up for more bug juice, please?" When she handed me the pitcher, half full, I assumed Patsy didn't want me to hear

Rory's accusations. But I already knew that my counselor wouldn't be able to protect me from Rory. What I didn't know was that no one would be able to guard me from my mother's past. *What secrets does Robin know?* I asked myself again as I carried the pitcher toward the front of the dining hall.

Nancy looked up as I walked by the owner's table. Her smile knifed through my anger and confusion. "You okay?" she mouthed. I nodded and turned away.

Clarence greeted me at the counter. "Hey, little lady. I was hoping I'd see you." His teeth were so white they looked fake. "My boys feel real bad about what happened at the lake." Clarence reached for the pitcher, my fingers still glued to its cool metal handle.

I swallowed the lump in my throat and took a long breath. "But Andy and Jed didn't do anything. They're nice boys."

"Well, they feel real bad, all the same." Clarence leaned forward on fingers like chocolate twigs. "Rory's bad news," he whispered. "As my mama used to say, 'You don't have to be a chicken to recognize a rotten egg.' It's just too bad she's in your cabin. But you know what, little lady? This place ain't no different from the rest of the world. You pays your money and you takes your chances. Just do the best with the cards in your hand. Ain't nothing else you can do now, is there?"

●

The heat wave ended, bringing a shot of crisp air and a flurry of letters. Bunks 7 and 8 sorted mail and delivered it, in brown accordion envelopes with elastic cords, to all the cabins. Older campers, eager for news, hung out on porch steps during rest hour.

Not Rory, though. She sat with feet pulled up on her bed, swishing her hand back and forth over newly painted toenails. Even Jessica, engrossed in reading a letter, ignored Rory's offer of Passion Pink polish.

"What's wrong with you retards?" Rory asked. "You've wasted this whole rest hour waiting for mail, as if what your parents write means a goddamn thing. Jesus, who cares about them, anyway?"

No answer. The only sound in the cabin was the ripping open of envelopes, the thumbing of stationery.

"Come on, girls." Rory wouldn't stop. "Time to have some fun before the bell rings. How 'bout a little smoking session behind the nature hut? I've got the cigs."

I glanced up from my father's letter as Rory flashed a pack of Salems. "Come on, Jess. Let's go."

Silence.

"Come on!" Rory tried again. "We're outta here."

I peeked at Rory as she slid into her flip-flops. For an instant, I almost felt sorry for her, the only one in the cabin with no word from home. But then I reminded myself who she was. I picked up my letter and read from the top:

Dear Amy,

I'm so glad you're having a great time. We knew you would.

The night swim sounds like lots of fun (and I won't tell Uncle Ed). But please don't do that again. Even a good swimmer like you should never go in without a counselor on duty.

Mom was disappointed to hear you signed up for tennis. She wants you to try as many new sports as you can. She said to tell you that the more things you try, the more you'll learn and the more people you'll get to know. But I don't see why you shouldn't play tennis. After all, you're there to have fun, and it sounds like that's just what you're doing.

Charlie's fine, though I know he misses you. The other day I found him in the hallway outside your room. When I asked what he was doing, he whispered your name. But don't worry. Mom says he's been very cooperative in the afternoons after summer school.

I love you, honey. Mom sends her love too. She's been really busy organizing closets and cleaning all the windows. She says she's getting an early start on fall cleaning. You know how your mother is—always looking ahead.

Keep having fun!

Love and kisses,
Dad

I pictured Charlie on the floor by my room: hands clasped around knees, elbows jutting like wings. Amy, how could you leave me? he probably wanted to know. But all that came out was a whispering of my name. How could you leave me with Mom? he might have thought. I made a building, but at cleanup time, I didn't put the blocks in order. And she told me to do it again—the right way now, Charlie, she ordered. Your father will be home soon. And dinner will be on the table, and the laundry will be folded, and the house will be clean. Everything in its place, and a place for every thing.

I read my father's letter again and saw my mother glancing at Charlie, curled into a ball on the hallway floor. I pictured her turning away, leaving him there all alone.

Why couldn't my mother just love us?

Chapter 7

I'm Not Fooling with You Now

My mother sat on my shoulder—watching me, warning me—in the dining hall. *It's a lot easier putting on weight than taking it off,* she whispered when Nancy announced we won an ice cream party for having the cleanest senior cabin. *You're not going to eat that cake, Amy. Not if you're having ice cream later.*

I longed to shove her off, to replace her with a mom who wouldn't demand I be thin, who wouldn't make me explain why I needed another bar of soap or tube of toothpaste. I wanted a home where I wouldn't have to ask my mother to unlock the closet in which she stashed shampoo and tissues, extra combs and toilet paper—parceling out each item as if it were rationed.

I scraped lines into the icing on the piece of cake I'd taken, then rested my fork at the edge of my plate.

"What's the matter, Amy?" Patsy asked. "Aren't you eatin' that cake?"

"I'll take it," Donnie said.

I pushed my plate over.

"Just a minute." Rory reached across the table. "Who said you could have it?"

Donnie tightened her fingers around the rim.

"Give it here," Rory demanded.

"No. I called it first." Everyone jerked to attention as Donnie's fingers curled around the plate, her knuckles whitening.

"Quit it, you two," Patsy said. "How 'bout you share it?"

"How 'bout you mind your own business?" Rory countered as Donnie shielded the plate with her arms.

"How 'bout you mind your manners, Rory, or no ice cream party for you."

"How 'bout you quit telling me what to do, Patsy. You're not my father." Rory stood up. She reached across the table, pushed Donnie's arms out of the way, and grabbed the plate. Campers applauded when it hit the floor.

Jessica giggled. "Nice play, Shakespeare."

Rory glared at me. "Clean it up, Amy. It was *your* plate."

"But it was *your* fault, Rory," Patsy said. "So go on and get some napkins to clean it with, or you'll be alone in the cabin tonight while we're making sundaes at Mr. Becker's house."

"You can't keep me from that party."

"Oh no? Just try me, gal."

I wanted to jump up and throw my arms around Patsy.

"It's your choice, Rory," she went on. "Clean up now, or no party later."

Rory slinked away. I was surprised she surrendered for an ice cream party. She took a couple of steps, then shot a grin back over her shoulder as if she had heard my thought. "You girls think I'd miss Patsy weaseling her way into Mr. Becker's house? No siree. I'm gonna be there when the sparks fly. Wouldn't wanna miss that show."

"And just what show are you talkin' 'bout?" Patsy asked.

Rory walked on, leaving Patsy's question in the air. But then she turned and looked at me, hatred glowing in her eyes. "And you, Amy Becker, you should've eaten your goddamn cake," she called. "This is *your* fault."

I didn't believe her then. This time I knew I wasn't to blame. It was my mother who had stopped me from eating that cake. Would I ever be able to get her off my shoulder?

●

We headed for the owner's house at the edge of camp, a hike beyond Nancy's cabin, past the bend in the lake. I walked with Donnie, behind Fran and Karen. Rory and Jessica took the lead. "Hi-ho. Hi-ho. To Mr. Becker's we go." They sang full out, as if Rory had dropped her anger on the trail, as if she had forgotten to pretend she was no longer young.

"I think her father beats her," Donnie whispered. "Beats her and makes her do stuff. Sex stuff. Maybe that's why she's so mean. But no one's supposed to know."

75

"Then how do *you* know?"

"Jess told me. Last year, visiting day. Rory's folks didn't come—they never do—and I actually felt kinda sorry for her, even though I really hate her guts. So I offered to share what my parents brought—peanut butter cookies, Twinkies, Devil Dogs—all sorts of good stuff. And Rory, she got so angry when I said I was sorry no one visited her, you know what she did? Threw my tin of cookies and ran out of the cabin. All those cookies, the one thing my mother baked special for me. And I was so mad I said I'd kill her. And I meant it too. But then Jessica—would you believe?—she calmed me down and told me about Rory's father. Said she wasn't supposed to tell anybody. Rory had sworn her to secrecy. But I guess Jess thought I deserved an explanation, since Rory sure wasn't gonna apologize."

From across the lake, a loon called as Patsy sneaked up on us. She put her arms around our waists. "Well, hey there, gals. Nearly scared me to death, that silly bird."

"Me too," Donnie said. "Those loony loons still make me jump, even after seven summers."

We walked on, our steps in sync, the only sound the pressing of pine needles, a giggle up ahead. "You're awful quiet, Amy." Patsy broke the silence that closed in on us. "What's on your mind?"

"Nothing much." I twirled my flashlight in figure eights as my stomach curled in on itself. How could a father abuse his own daughter?

"Sure you're okay?"

"Yeah, fine." I knew not to talk about what Donnie had said. Patsy loped ahead to Fran and Karen.

"The way I see it," Donnie went on, "camp's the only place where Rory can strike back. Know what I mean? Feel powerful. And this summer she's sure taking it out on you. So I figured you deserved an explanation too."

I nodded, not realizing Donnie would miss my gesture in the dark.

"Can I ask you something?" Donnie said.

"Sure."

"Why'd you take it from her? The initiation, I mean. Why didn't you scream while we were still in the cabin, or...I don't know...do something to stop her?"

I had no answer. Only a picture in my mind: a little girl on Daddy's lap. *Merrily, merrily, do as you're told. Do as you're told, Amy. Do as you're told.* Memories. Images. *And don't you ever talk back to your mother. Her life hasn't been easy. She's lost so much. She deserves whatever happiness we can give her.* A blip of my mother plumping cushions on the sofa. *Stay in your room, Amy.*

Secrets of my mother's past. What had she hidden from me? What had she lost? Cousin Robin seemed to know. She had dangled my mother's secrets on the tennis court. Yet I had no idea what they could be.

"Why didn't you try to stop the initiation?" Donnie asked again.

"I...I'm not sure." I shivered as we walked in silence toward our ice cream celebration.

●

Aunt Helen and Uncle Ed lived in The Lodge, a great stone house in a clearing in the pines. "Welcome! Welcome, girls!"

Aunt Helen motioned us in. I was grateful to be lumped with the girls now, having dreaded my aunt's singling me out as family.

Cool air attacked us as we entered the humongous main room, a testament to pre-air-conditioning, old-fashioned construction. I rubbed the goose bumps on my arms, impossible to smooth in the presence of a moose head mounted high above the massive stone fireplace.

Moose eyes seemed to follow me as I studied the two staircases flanking the room. They led to a balcony. I strained to see what was up there. Doors. Lots of doors upstairs—bedrooms and bathrooms, I assumed. Nothing but a kitchen and the main room downstairs, with Mr. Moose standing guard.

Aunt Helen flitted around as if she thought she was supposed to be doing something but didn't know what. We stood in pairs, not knowing what we were supposed to do either. No chairs to sink into. Only an upright piano in the corner, angled under one of the landings, a long table with bowls and sundae fixings under the other, and a bear rug—head and all—by the fireplace. Were we supposed to sit on the floor? On the bear?

"Uncle Ed's not back yet," Aunt Helen jabbered. "He went to get the ice cream. Drove on over to the general store for you girls, and honest to goodness, you certainly do deserve it, what with you winning senior inspection and all. Though I do wish Robin and her bunkmates could be here too. But anyhoodle, I've got your party set up over there." Aunt Helen pointed to the table as I glanced to see if anyone else had caught her *anyhoodle.*

Jessica's hand covered her mouth. Rory slapped it down. "Behave, Jess," she said too loudly. "It's rude to giggle when Mrs. Becker's nice enough to give us this little shindig."

"Well, it's my pleasure, girls. So make yourselves comfortable. *Mi casa es su casa*, as they say in...ummm...Spain. Isn't that right? So let's see...." Aunt Helen cupped her chin and looked around, as if noticing for the first time this room devoid of furniture. "Why don't you girls get settled on the bear rug."

"Why, thank you, Mrs. Becker," Patsy said. "It's right nice of you to have us over this evening."

"No problem at all. So sit down, girls. Ed should be back in a jiff."

Rory pulled Jessica to the bear. They sat by its head, facing the door, Rory's legs spread-eagled around the bear's skull. She stroked it as if petting a dog. The rest of us scrunched like a litter of pups toward the back of the rug. Once we were seated, cross-legged, Patsy settled herself behind Rory. I noticed my counselor tuck her legs to the side, like a girl in a meadow, waiting for someone to bring her a picnic basket.

Aunt Helen moved to the table. She fiddled with plastic spoons, rearranged paper napkins. "Now where in the dickens is that man?" she muttered. "One little errand—ice cream and sodas—and he's gone for over an hour. Probably chatting with every counselor who's out for the evening. Why it's a wonder that man ever gets anything done with all the gabbing he does."

"I think she means flirting," Rory said, twisting to face Patsy, who addressed Aunt Helen. "Don't you fret now, Mrs. Becker. I'm sure Mr. Becker'll be arrivin' right shortly."

"Thank you, dear. And please, call me Helen."

"Yes, Helen. I'm sure he'll be along soon."

"I'm just sorry to keep you girls waiting." Aunt Helen stacked and restacked bowls, picked up plastic spoons, and fanned them in a paper cup.

"No problem, ma'am," Rory said. "We don't mind waiting for your husband to get back. No siree. Not one bit."

Someone must have suggested we sing. As if a leader raised a baton, we started in the same breath:

> *Swing low, sweet chariot,*
> *comin' for to carry me home.*
> *Swing low, sweet chariot,*
> *comin' for to carry me home.*

We didn't hear Uncle Ed's car pull up behind the house. We didn't hear him walk around front. "Ah, the voices of angels," he said, toeing open the door. "I could listen all night."

"What in the world took you so long?" Aunt Helen called from the corner by the party table. "I swear, I've got a good mind to do all the errands myself from now on. Leave you here next time to entertain our guests."

"Why, that would be a pleasure, my dear." Uncle Ed hugged grocery bags as he crossed the room toward Aunt Helen. "An absolute pleasure," he said with a wink as he passed our huddle. "Keep singing, girls." He unloaded treats onto the table behind which Aunt Helen stationed herself. "The voices of angels. No sweeter sound in the world."

We worked our way through "Swing Low, Sweet Chariot" and "Joshua Fit The Battle Of Jericho." After the last *walls came tumblin' down*, Aunt Helen invited us to step up for ice cream.

Uncle Ed dashed from the table. "You too," he said to Patsy, offering his hands to guide her from the rug. A familiar gesture, followed by a flicker of memory: a picnic. A long time ago. Before Charlie. Robin and I sit on the grass. My parents on a blanket with Aunt Helen and Uncle Ed. My uncle gets up and holds his hands out to my mother, helps her to her feet.

Now I watched him help Patsy. "Why thank you, Mr. Becker," she said, her drawl suddenly making my stomach flip.

"Such formality. My goodness, Patsy. Call me Ed."

"And the show begins," Rory said.

We lined up for our second dessert of the day—two too many, my mother would have pointed out.

"Ed, come on back here and help me scoop this," Aunt Helen said. "It's hard as a rock. If you were going to take your time at the store, least you could've done is pick up the ice cream first, let it soften a bit while you talked yourself out. Now how in the world do you expect me to serve this?"

"Allow me," Uncle Ed offered.

Aunt Helen moved from behind the table.

"Why not let me help, Mr. Becker? Ed." Patsy pushed in next to him.

Aunt Helen stalked over to the bear rug as if on a mission.

"What?" Jessica asked when Rory punched her arm.

"Nothing. Forget it," Rory answered. "What flavors you got there, Mr. B.?"

I turned to watch my aunt fluff the rug as if it were a quilt. She straightened the bear's head. It drooped to the side. She righted it. It fell again.

Aunt Helen seemed to work hard at ignoring her husband and Patsy at the party table, where we made sundaes. Chocolate, vanilla, and strawberry ice cream. Marshmallow topping. Chocolate syrup. Whipped cream in a can. Nuts. Colored sprinkles. Maraschino cherries.

Girls giggled as they sprayed Redi-Whip like shaving cream. They built their concoctions—the bigger, the better—crowning mountains of ice cream with syrup and nuts. Pure joy. I wanted that: joy without *what if*. What if my mother saw me eating this? What if I poured on extra syrup, took more nuts?

"Hey, Patsy," Rory said, sucking whipped cream off her fingers. "Mmmm. Yummy. Want some?"

"Go sit down, Rory. I'm not fooling with you now."

"Who's fooling?"

"I think you've got enough there in your dish, young lady," Uncle Ed said. "Sit down and eat."

"But I just thought Patsy might like this, Mr. B. And a cherry too. A nice big juicy one." Rory ogled Uncle Ed as she pulled a cherry from its stem with her teeth.

"See, that's what I mean, Ed," Patsy said. "That's the behavior."

"Wait a minute. You've been talking about me?"

"What Patsy and I talk about is none of your business, young lady. But I'll tell you this: You clean up your act, or no camp store for a week."

"Come on now, Mr. B. You wouldn't take that away from me," Rory said, drawing out each word. A smile played at her mouth. "Not a nice man like you."

"I sure would. And you keep this up, I'll take away rest hour privileges too."

"Ah, come on, Mr. B. Just because I'm on to you, you wouldn't deny me privileges. Just 'cause I see what's going on here. Such a nice, handsome man like you, you wouldn't want me to be sad now, would you?"

"Keep going, Rory, and you won't have to worry about privileges. You keep up this inappropriate behavior, and I'll send you home."

Yes! Keep it up! Send her home! I wanted to shout.

Rory's smile grew in defiance. "You just try and kick me out of camp, Mr. B., and you'll see how fast other parents get wind of what you did—sending me home for no reason at all, no reason except maybe…maybe I turn you on. That's it, isn't it? That's what this is about. Scary thought, though. A girl your daughter's age. Your daughter's friend, in fact. Maybe you want time alone with pretty Patsy and me together. How does that sound, Mr. B.?"

We clustered in silence around the table, Rory's words more seductive than ice cream. "What's she saying about Patsy?" Aunt Helen called, giving up on the bear.

"Nothing, dear," Uncle Ed said, his voice as sugared as sundaes. "Nothing for you to concern yourself with, Helen. Just Rory talking nonsense, that's all."

Rory slammed down her bowl. I watched whipped cream topple to the table as if in slow motion. "You call that nonsense?" she said. "Well, I gotta differ with you there, Mr. B. Ask anyone. Go ahead. Anyone with eyes can see you're a ladies' man. And just wait till I tell my parents. Why, you won't even know what hit you when the word gets out and you start losing campers. Yes indeedy. Great first season, huh, Mr. B.?"

Aunt Helen marched to the table. "What's she talking about, Ed?"

"Nothing, Helen. She's finished. Aren't you, Rory?" Uncle Ed's red face belied the calm in his voice. "Because I'll tell you this: This is your last warning. You clean up your act or I *will* send you home, and I'm sure you don't want me to do that."

"You don't know anything about what I want."

"That's not so. I know you don't want to get kicked out of camp. But one false move, Rory, and I'll do it."

Rory lowered her head, then spoke in a voice filled with sadness. "Please, Mr. Becker. I'm sorry. Please don't send me home."

"Okay, gals," Patsy said. "Y'all finish making your sundaes and go on enjoy 'em before they turn to mush."

I took three scoops, one of each flavor, and every topping on the table—including marshmallow, which I don't even like. To hell with *what-ifs*. I grabbed a spoon and joined Donnie on the bear rug.

"Watch it now, girls," Aunt Helen said as she handed out napkins. "No drips. Right? Heaven only knows how to clean a bear."

"Very carefully," Jessica said. "Very carefully. Get it?"

Everyone smiled but Rory. She sat strangely silent, head bowed, shoulders hunched.

I ate my sundae and thought about what might happen to her at home. How could a father abuse his own daughter?

Chapter 8

An Eye for an Eye

Sometimes during rest hour, Erin and I visited Nancy in the head counselor's cabin, and sometimes we went to the boathouse. Erin brought whatever treats her mother had stashed in her latest care package: candy hidden in a stationery box, gum sealed up in envelopes, cookies tucked into T-shirts.

"You know, parents send stuff like this all the time," Erin told me the first day she showed up with snacks. She handed me a Sugar Daddy. "My mother hides the good stuff so it's not obvious. You know, 'cause we're really not supposed to have food in the cabins."

"I didn't know that."

"Yep. No junk food allowed. Except on visiting day, when everyone eats like crazy. But tell your mother she can still send whatever you want. She just has to make sure her care packages don't look like they're filled with food."

"Okay. Thanks." I popped the Sugar Daddy into my mouth. Care packages. Someone would have to care about you to send them. I shut my eyes and savored the sweet Sugar Daddy.

●

Erin and I headed to the boathouse separately the day after the ice cream party. Why give Rory a chance to sneer at our friendship? Why risk Robin seeing us?

"Better not let your cousin know we're meeting today," Erin said, lagging on her way out of breakfast that morning. "I mean, Robin's getting as bad as Rory, always putting her nose into everyone's business and sticking with Rory as if they were glued together. No offense, but it's hard to believe you're related."

So Erin noticed it too—how Robin and Rory had become buddies. How could Robin be the same girl who used to invite me to her birthday parties? And why did she seem to hate me now?

Erin and I sat on the boathouse floor that afternoon, our backs to canoes racked against the wall. I tried to tuck my legs to the side rather than cross them. Patsy would manage to sit like a lady, I was sure. My mother too. They would assume the perfect pose no matter how hard the damp floorboards pushed against their limbs. I wriggled to find comfort and poise, then gave up. Why chafe my thigh when my mother wasn't there to see me? I crossed my legs as the story about Rory and her father burst out. "But don't tell anyone," I said. "Donnie said no one's supposed to know."

"Well, actually, I heard that rumor last summer," Erin said.

"But doesn't it bother you?"

"I don't know. Guess I don't think about it much or I would've already told you. I mean, why should I even think about that? Why think about something that might not even be true about someone I hate to think about in the first place?" Erin paused to stare at an army of ants working its way up a paddle. "But what I do think about," she went on, "is what Rory did to you. And what really makes me angry is she gets away with it. And she'll do it again and again till someone stops her. So maybe that's what we ought to be talking about. It's time for revenge, I say. Don't get mad; get even."

"What do you mean?"

"Maybe we should get her before she tries anything again." Erin twirled a pigtail with her index finger. "It's like I told Nancy: I'd rather eat worms than cave in to Rory all summer."

"So what can we do?"

"Give her a taste of her own medicine. That's what I say. Make Rory suffer for a change." A smile crinkled Erin's face, visible in the thin line of sunlight that snuck through the boat-house door, which we always left cracked open. She threw a playful punch at my shoulder. "We're smart. We'll think of something."

"But last night, when Uncle Ed threatened to kick her out of camp, you should have seen her."

"*What?* He did *what?*"

I told Erin what had happened the night before.

"That's great. I can't believe you didn't tell me sooner. So how's this? We get Rory to do something really bad when your uncle's around. Maybe at the Saginaw social." She twirled her pigtails until I thought her hair would spring from her head. "Holy moly! We could get her sent home."

"I don't know. You didn't see how Rory looked when Uncle Ed said he'd kick her out." I surprised myself with this hesitation. Of course I wanted Rory kicked out. Sometimes I still wished she would drown in the lake. Every time I looked at her now, I imagined pushing her off the float and waiting for the snapping turtle to strike. But even so, I didn't want her to suffer at the hands of her father.

"Listen, Ame." There it was: my nickname, the bridge to friendship. Best friends for the next six weeks. Maybe getting even with Rory wouldn't be wrong, no matter what might happen to her. After all, she had threatened Erin and the others when they left my initiation. Maybe it was my turn now to do something for them: help them go after Rory. An eye for an eye. That old Hammurabi Code I'd learned about in social studies.

"Listen," Erin said again. "We need to make a plan. The Saginaw social's coming up. Whaddaya say we get our gang together tomorrow at rest hour and work it out?"

"What gang?"

"You know: you and me, Donnie, Fran, and Karen. The ones who turned on Rory during that stupid initiation. And Paula too, from my cabin. We'll meet here in the boathouse. Rory'll never find us. You and I are the only ones who use this place. So tomorrow then. I'll spread the word. Rory watches you more than me, so I'll get everyone here. You just show up during rest hour. Okay?"

An eye for an eye. I couldn't say no.

●

"Leave it to Erin," Donnie said when she caught up to me on the way to the boathouse the next day. "She's right. Don't get mad; get even. And it's about time we get even with Rory."

Getting mad I could handle. But getting even? When I thought about Rory's father, I still really wasn't sure. A chill worked through me although heat pushed down on us again, reminding me of the weather on the morning I'd left for camp. My father in his T-shirt: "Think I'll turn on the air conditioner. Maybe a little air'll get in here." My mother holding him back: "We'll be gone before it cools down." Why did my father always hand her the reins? Was it her looks, her perfect figure? Something to do with sex?

I gagged at the idea as I tried to flick my mother off my shoulder. *Two wrongs don't make a right,* my mother whispered in my ear as Donnie opened the boathouse door. Was my mother telling me not to go after Rory? Would she say I had gotten what I deserved: punishment for being me, for not being pretty like she was? For not being sexy like Robin, like Rory? Sure, they might not have attacked me if I had big hair and polished nails. Yet it was my mother who wouldn't let me use rollers; my mother who told me I couldn't wear polish if I still picked at my cuticles. I heard her voice again: *Two wrongs don't make a right, Amy.*

Whose code held the truth, my mother's or Hammurabi's? And what about the Takawanda code? The law of the jungle: Eat or be eaten.

"Okay, you guys," Erin said as we settled in a circle on the dank floor. "First we need a secret word."

"What for?" Paula asked.

"For when we're at the social," Erin explained, "which is when I think we should get Rory in trouble. We say the word, and bingo, we get her."

An eye for an eye. Hammurabi was right. So what if Rory's father would abuse her? I couldn't keep letting her get me. Camp was a jungle; I'd play by the law. Eat or be eaten. "Think about what Rory does," I said.

"Mean things."

"Sexy things."

"Right." I enjoyed the limelight for a change, enjoyed ignoring my mother's *two wrongs don't make a right* mantra. "And when Rory does those things," I continued, "she roars."

"That's great, Ame." Erin picked up my thought. "She roars like a—"

"Lion!" we shouted.

"Holy moly! That's it," Erin said. "Lion. Our secret word, the code for our plan. Now let's work on it."

Paula spoke first. "All we have to do is arrange for Mr. Becker to find Rory doing something wrong, something bad enough to get her kicked out."

"That shouldn't be hard," Donnie said. "Rory does bad things all the time. We just have to figure out how to get her to do it when Mr. Becker's around."

"Do *it*?" Karen said.

Fran snickered. "*It*, as in sex?"

I didn't understand this focus on sex. I expected that from Rory's gang, but not from mine. Yet even Erin grinned. "Now we're cooking," she said, pulling the rubber bands from her hair. "So here's the deal. The Saginaw social will be in The Lodge. What if we get Rory to sneak upstairs with a boy? Then we'll get Mr. Becker to find her there doing something naughty."

"Doing *it*?"

"Having sex?"

"Well, she doesn't have to go all the way," Erin explained. "Just has to have her shirt open or something with a boy in a room where she's not supposed to be."

"And how do we arrange that?" Paula asked.

"Well, we could tell Rory we're sorry we haven't been getting along better, and—"

"Or maybe I could tell her I'm sorry I got her in trouble in the dining hall over that stupid piece of cake," Donnie said. "I could say I'm making it up to her by arranging a little privacy for her and the boy of her choice."

"A piece for a piece," Karen added. "That's great."

Fran elbowed her. "That's disgusting!"

I couldn't admit I didn't fully understand what they were saying. If the girls found out how little I knew about this type of stuff, they might not want me in their group. I heard my mother's voice again: *You don't know anything, Amy. Nothing.* I realized she was right. I didn't know anything. And if I admitted it, I'd have no one.

"It'll never work," Paula said. "First, we won't be able to get Rory upstairs without anyone seeing. And second, even if we do, how're we gonna get Mr. Becker up there to find her?"

If I helped with the plan, they would like me even better. If I helped with the plan, they wouldn't know how stupid I was. I blurted out a better idea. "Maybe we could get Rory to go outside with a boy while we block the door so no one sees them leave, and then we could tell Uncle Ed we hear noises or something. Get him to go out and find them."

"Ame, you're brilliant," Erin said. "So Operation Lion, ready to go. Amy and I can work out the details. The rest of you will just block the door when we say the word. So...the bell's gonna ring soon. You guys go back to senior camp while Amy and I finalize the plan. And remember: top secret."

"No problem." Donnie spoke for all of us. "The lion is caged."

"Not to worry," Erin told me after the others left, closing the door behind them. "You and me, Ame. We'll make it work. Pretty soon Rory will have roared her last roar."

Erin put a hand on my shoulder as we moseyed toward the door. It opened before we got there. "Well, look who's here, Ed," Patsy purred. "Mr. Becker and I were just takin' a little walk, and we thought we saw some gals headin' out from here. So what are y'all doin' in the boathouse?"

"Nothing. Just goofing off," Erin answered.

Uncle Ed's eyes fixed on mine. "This boathouse is off-limits, Amy. I don't expect to see you here again. And by the way, I just spoke to your father. He says there hasn't been much mail from you. So I suggest you use rest hour for letter-writing from now on. That's the least you could do for your parents and your brother."

Chapter 9

It's Just a Package

Rory pulled a note from our mail folder. "Well, lookie here. It says there's a package for Amy." She held the paper high in the air. "Wonder what Mommy and Daddy sent their precious little girl."

I knew what it was—certainly not a care package from my mother. I had asked Dad to send my light blue Bermudas with my blue and white shirt, and my navy pedal pushers with the madras top I had begged my mother to buy for my birthday last fall. I'd heard Rory and Jessica planning their outfits for the Saginaw social as if choosing from a closet of possibilities. All I had were my green camp shorts and Takawanda shirts. And though Erin had told me not to worry—I could borrow something from her—I wanted my own clothes.

"Ease up, Rory," Donnie said. "Just give us the package slip."

"Us? You and Amy are an us now? Well, la-de-da. Always figured you had better taste, Donnie-girl."

"Just give it to them," Fran muttered.

"Oh, stuff it." Rory wouldn't quit.

"You don't need that paper, Amy," Karen said. "Just go to the gatehouse and tell them you're picking up a package. No one'll ask for a slip."

"Is that so?" Rory still held the paper as she approached my bed. "Well, what if I told you, Amy Becker, that they won't give you your package without this ticket? The rules are different this year, girls: no tickie, no washie. Catch my drift?" Rory waved the paper like a flag. "And look who's got the slip."

"Not anymore you don't." Donnie moved behind Rory and swiped the form, then raced outside. "Amy, meet me in Bunk 10," she called from the stoop.

Rory leaned forward, hands braced on my bed. Her eyes gripped mine. I looked down.

"What's the matter? Never had a staring contest?"

My vocal cords stuck.

"Ah, cat got your tongue again, I see. Well, I've got ways to make you talk, Amy Becker. After your friends leave, that is." Rory relaxed her hold on my bed and turned toward Fran and Karen. "Time for you to fly the coop so Amy and I can have a private little powwow."

"Yeah," Jessica said, "a powwow with someone who won't even talk. You're a riot, Rory."

"Shut your trap, Jess. You're starting to get on my nerves." Rory looked at Fran and Karen. "And you two, didn't you hear me? Or are you both deaf? It's no wonder you side with Amy: You're deaf and she's mute. What a bunch of retards in this cabin."

My stomach twisted like a washcloth. If my getting a package was enough to force Rory's rage, there was nothing I could control. Who knew what she would do to me if Fran and Karen left? "You didn't cooperate during your initiation, Amy Becker," Rory had whispered several times. Now I needed the other girls to protect me. *Don't go. Please don't go.*

They stayed on their beds as if they heard my silent plea.

"What's the matter with you two?" Rory asked. "I told you to get out."

Fran and Karen didn't move.

"Well then, just remember: You cross me now, I'll cross you later. So get the hell outta here. Go!"

The lion had roared. Fran and Karen bolted from the cabin. Rory leaned forward again, tightening her hands on my bed. "So finally, Amy Becker, it's just us. Just you and me and Jess. And you've got a choice to make. You either listen to your so-called friends, who don't know squat about anything, or you listen to me. So which is it? Me or them?"

My voice still wouldn't come.

"Jesus, girl. I said you've got a choice to make. So make it already. I'm not gonna waste all rest hour waiting for you to wise up."

Donnie saved me when she opened the door. "Give her a break, Rory. It's just a package. What's the big deal?" Donnie paused for a second, expecting an answer that didn't come. Then she summoned me from the doorway. "Let's go, Amy. I'll walk you to the gatehouse."

"Time to choose," Rory said again, her face too close, the tuna salad from lunch heavy on her breath.

Fear pressed on my chest. I pulled in air as I closed my notepad on the beginning of a letter to Charlie, the first in days. "I'm coming, Donnie."

"Wrong choice, you little twerp," Rory sneered.

I jumped into my sneakers, not stopping to tie them, and ran from the cabin.

Dear Amy,

I hope you're not disappointed with this package, but Mom said your red dress and party shoes are more appropriate for a dance than the clothes you asked for, and when it comes to looks, your mother's the expert. So I'm sure you'll be the belle of the ball. Please write to us after the dance and tell us all about it.

Speaking of writing, we haven't gotten much mail from you. Mom says that means you're having so much fun there's no time to write. "No news is good news," she says. But I think Charlie would like it if I had some letters to read to him at night. So please find a little time to remember your brother.

Write to us about the tennis tournament. Have you played any matches? Maybe you and I can hit when we come for visiting day.

Uncle Ed tells me the season has gotten off to a great start. I'm so pleased we were able to send you.

I love you, honey. Mom sends her love too. Keep having fun.

Love and kisses,
Dad

Not a word about Charlie, except my father's letdown in my not having written to him more. It wasn't only my mother I had disappointed. It was my father now. And Charlie too.

I stashed the red dress and party shoes in the bottom of my trunk, where I kept the extra bath towels my mother had insisted I bring. "See, Ed knows nothing about running a camp," she had said as we packed. "They should have put more towels on this list. What if the laundry loses one of yours, and the other one's wet? Then what?"

As I hid the "appropriate outfit" in my trunk, my mother perched on my shoulder again. *You're not going to wear the dress, Amy? Then you'll find out the hard way that boys like girls who look like ladies.*

●

"Not to worry," Erin said the next day as we walked toward Nancy's cabin during rest hour—even though I knew I should be writing to Charlie. "I told you, you can borrow anything you want. And anyhow, what we wear doesn't matter. The only thing that matters is the plan. And I think *Lion's* gonna work. It'll be a cold day in hell when Rory hurts us again." Erin draped her arm around me. "And just think what fun we'll have once she's gone."

By the time we got to Nancy's, Erin had convinced me. Camp without Rory. I couldn't help smiling.

"You look like the cat that swallowed the canary," Nancy called from in front of her cabin. "Let me in on it, ladies. What's the good news?"

"Nothing, Nance," Erin answered. "You know, girl talk. Nothing special."

"Oh, come on. Tell me." Nancy motioned us in.

"We can't," Erin said with a grin. "It's a secret. Right, Amy?"

I nodded.

"Well, okay. It's just good to see you two having fun. That's what camp's all about: fun and friendship. Secrets too, I suppose." She sat between us on her bed and went on. "I'm just glad there hasn't been any more trouble. But if there ever is, I want you to come to me right away." She paused, maybe trying to guess our secret. "And don't even think about doing anything silly, like getting back at Rory. Though I know you two would never hurt anyone, even if she deserves it. Erin Hollander and Amy Becker, the nicest seniors in Takawanda history."

Erin and I inched to the very edge of the bed and glanced at each other. This time neither of us smiled. Was Erin thinking the same thing I was: that maybe we should backpedal on our plan to get Rory?

Before the bell rang, Nancy walked us out, arms around us. My stomach flipped. I knew I didn't merit this affection, Nancy's confidence in my judgment and the trust in her eyes.

"I'm thinking about what Nancy said," Erin told me as we headed back to senior camp. "But I still want to go ahead with the plan. Look, Ame. Nancy practically said that Rory deserves it. And we already have friendship and secrets. That's two out of Nancy's three. So now all we have to do is get rid of Rory, and we'll finally have fun. I say we go for it."

No backpedaling, I realized. *Lion* was still on.

Dear Charlie,

I'm so sorry I haven't sent you more letters, but there's not much time to write. During rest hour I'm always busy with my friends, and there's almost no other free time. But I think of you every day, and I miss you, buddy.

Guess what? We won an ice cream party for having the cleanest cabin in senior camp. It was so much fun! We went to The Lodge, where Uncle Ed and Aunt Helen live. Their house is in the woods, and they have a bear rug and a moose head above the fireplace. It's not at all like their house in Westchester.

Dad wanted me to write about the tennis tournament. It's called a round-robin, which is pretty funny since cousin Robin signed up for it too. Anyhow, everyone in the tournament plays everyone else, and then there are playoff matches. My first match is tomorrow. Jody, the head tennis counselor, thinks I have a chance of making it all the way to the finals. Wish me luck!

The other news is there's a social this week with a boys camp. I'm really excited. Everyone's talking about sharing outfits, so I'm not sure what I'll end up wearing. But tell Mom and Dad I appreciate the dress.

Well, I gotta scoot, scoot, skedaddle. Even though I'm having a great time, I miss you, buddy, and I love you so much.

Love,
Amy

●

The temperature rose above ninety on the afternoon of the tennis match. Regular activities were canceled. "It's Miami Beach Day, campers," Nancy announced at the end of lunch. A loud cheer rolled through the dining hall. "Seniors with scheduled tennis matches, please meet with Jody," Nancy continued. "And I'll see everyone at the lake after rest hour."

Erin raced over when Nancy dismissed our group. "Miami Beach Day means we get the whole afternoon at the lake. So don't let Jody convince you to play your match. Just tell her you'll play tomorrow."

How could I let Erin know Jody wouldn't have to convince me? Time at the lake might mean another battle, another chance for Rory to attack. I had chosen sides, racing off with Donnie to collect my package. Now, regardless of the swarm of counselors at the waterfront, Rory would be out to punish me. The lake might be just the spot. Even if the temperature reached one hundred, I'd choose tennis over swimming.

"I'll do what I can," I lied as I headed to the front of the dining hall, where Jody huddled with Nancy.

Mine wasn't the only match scheduled for that afternoon, but it was the only one played. I lucked out with my opponent, Marcy Bernstein from Bunk 8, who was squeamish about fish. Even tiny minnows made her scream. Shelly Davis, the waterfront director, practically had to push Marcy in for instructional swim.

"Okay, ladies," Jody said when Marcy and I told her we wanted to play. "How about right after rest hour? And bring your canteens. You'll need plenty of water."

●

The rules for the tennis match were simple: The winner would be the first player to take eight games, by a margin of two. Before I knew it, I had won the first three. Focused on the tennis ball, I forgot my father's disappointment in my not writing more and my mother's warning about appropriate dress. I saw the ball come toward me and forgot about Charlie too. But I didn't forget Rory, whose face I saw in every shot. Rory, who in the two weeks since my initiation would say, "Time for a swim, Amy Becker," whenever we changed into our bathing suits. Rory, who would race toward me in the lake whenever the counselors turned their heads, who'd call out, "Never played doctor, Amy Becker?"

Hit the ball, Amy. Smack it hard. It's Rory—her nasty tone, her constant threats. *Time to choose, Amy. Me or them?*

What would Rory do to me if the plan didn't work, if she guessed we were out to get her in trouble?

"Take a drink, girls," Jody said when I led four games to two. "And refill your canteens. I don't want you passing out from the heat."

Back on the court, I told myself to stay focused. But my mind wandered to the Saginaw social. What if the plan worked? We'd win. Rory would lose. Yet I knew what might be going on in her house. Though I couldn't forget what she had done to me, and it didn't matter if I'd ever forgive her, I wasn't sure I'd be able to forgive myself for getting her sent back to her father.

An eye for an eye. Pretty convincing. Eat or be eaten. But my mother continued to storm through my head. *Two wrongs don't make a right, Amy.* Did that mean I shouldn't fight? Just go forward like my mother, try to tune out the past?

"That's four apiece," Marcy announced after taking some games.

Focus. Concentrate, I warned myself. *You can't lose the first match—not after Jody said you could make it to the finals.*

"Four-all," Marcy said again as she bounced the ball before serving.

"Good return!" a male voice called when I hit a winner. Andy and Jed waved racquets as they crossed the lawn. "We didn't think anyone would be here all afternoon on account of the schedule change. Jed and I just wanted to hit for a spell."

"No problem," Jody said. "But play quietly. There's a match going on."

"A m-m-match? S-sorry. We d-d-didn't know."

"It's fine, fellas. Just use an upper court."

"Could we...maybe...could we watch?" Andy asked.

Jody left it to us. "I don't mind," Marcy said.

"Me neither." Why not, I thought. They're nice boys, nice enough to have left my initiation. And my father always said I played well to an audience.

The boys applauded my good shots—louder, it seemed, than they did Marcy's. Each "Great shot, Amy!" made me hit the ball harder. I forgot about Rory and the plan and *what-ifs*. I forgot about my mother. All that mattered was the strike of the ball.

I won four straight games to close out the match. "You're a good player," Andy told me. "You too, Marcy. So do you girls want to stay and hit with Jed and me for a while?"

"I think they've had enough," Jody answered for us. "It's time for a swim."

"No. Please, Jody," Marcy begged. "Please let us stay."

"But it's hot as blazes. Don't you want to swim?"

My fear of Rory at the lake came back like a punch to my gut. "No, please. I'd rather play tennis."

"All right," Jody agreed. "But not too much longer."

"Okay then," Andy said. He smiled and took my arm, claiming his partner. "Let's play."

My face flushed with victory. *See, Mom. It doesn't matter what I wear. Andy likes me just the way I am.*

●

I couldn't wait to tell Erin: how when Andy smiled, my heart pounded double time; how when we won the few games Jody let us play against Jed and Marcy, Andy's touch on my shoulder made my whole arm tingle. But by the time I got to the lake and swam to the floats, the whistle blew for campers to head in.

Rory trailed Erin and me to our towels—so close I couldn't speak. Had Marcy already told her friends about tennis? And had they told Rory, even before swimming ended? She lingered on the path, seeking signs of my time with Andy. I was certain of it. Another thing to tease me about.

"Have fun at tennis?" Rory asked as she watched me in the cabin.

"It was okay," I said, hiding my enthusiasm, hoping to disabuse Rory of her notion that something had happened. Yet as I spoke, I still felt Andy's hand on my shoulder and pictured the way he had chosen me as his partner. No, Rory wouldn't snuff the joy out of this day. I wouldn't let her suffocate me now. Looking toward Bunk 10, I wanted air and a chance to talk with Erin.

But all evening, and the next morning too, every time I got close to Erin, Rory squeezed in closer. "I have to talk to you," I finally whispered to Erin after breakfast.

"Me too," she answered quietly. "I heard about Andy. Meet me at the boathouse. Rest hour."

I wanted to take Donnie's job clearing the lunch table. But Rory would know something was up. Yet I longed to see Andy. He'd be waiting at the pass-through, I imagined. His hand would brush mine when I'd set down the sandwich platter. He'd smile, and I would forget Rory, forget our plan for the Saginaw social, forget my mother even.

Erin beat me to the boathouse, but she wasn't waiting inside. "Shhhh," she warned, an index finger to her lips. She cupped an ear with her other hand and leaned in close to the door.

I tiptoed next to her. Giggles from inside. Then a moaning breath. Hushed voices. Who was in there?

We heard the floor creak. Erin grabbed me and we ran toward our cabins. "Who do you think it was?" Erin asked as we approached senior camp.

My thoughts were all tangled up. Was someone having sex in the boathouse? Part of me wanted to know, and part of me couldn't stand to think about it. "Who cares?" I said, sounding meaner than intended.

"Fine. We don't have to talk about it if you don't want to. But tell me about Andy. That's what you wanted to talk about, right?"

"Forget it. It's not important."

Erin socked my arm. "Oh, come on. Tell me."

"Really, there's nothing to tell." I decided to keep Andy to myself—at least for a while. I wouldn't talk about him, and I wouldn't think about whatever had been going on in the boathouse. No outer world in; no inner world out. It worked for my mother. I would make it work for me too.

Chapter 10

The Laughingstock of Senior Camp

The day of the social, I still didn't have an outfit. "Not to worry," Erin said as we left the dining hall after breakfast. "We'll figure it out at rest hour."

During archery I could barely pull an arrow from the quiver. Could my mother be right about what to wear? Absolutely not, I decided. Yet I heard her voice as I drew the bowstring to my chin. *Wear the dress, Amy, or you'll be sorry.* Sorry about what? That I wouldn't be asked to dance? That I wouldn't have a boyfriend?

The other girls knew what they would wear to please the Saginaw boys. They'd spent days choosing from assorted clothing. Donnie had tried on multiple outfits, asking my opinion as she mixed and matched Bermudas and blouses.

"Oh, like it really matters what Amy thinks," Rory said. "You still don't get it, Donnie-girl, do you? No boy's gonna waste his time on you, and Amy's opinion isn't gonna help that. And anyhow, no one gives a damn what either of you wears. Come on. Andy and Jed weren't even interested in seeing Amy with no clothes on at all." Rory stroked her chin. "Though now that I think about it, it might be fun to see Amy's outfit. So time for a little fashion show. How 'bout it, Amy Becker?"

"Why don't you ease up on her already?" Donnie jumped in before I could figure out what to say. "You just said nobody cares what Amy and I wear. So forget it, Rory. You're right. It doesn't matter."

"Good. I'm glad we got that cleared up, that part about my being right. But you know, Donnie-girl, I must admit, I am just a teensy bit curious. So let's see, Amy. What outfit have you planned for turning the boys on?"

How could I tell her I didn't know, that I'd have to borrow something from Erin? When cornered about the package my parents had sent, I'd told Rory it was sheets and towels—anything to get her off my back.

"She hasn't decided what she's wearing yet," Donnie said.

"What's the matter, Amy?" Rory teased. "Cat got your tongue again? You need ol' Donnie-girl to talk for you now?"

"Leave her alone," Donnie answered for me.

"Well, I'll be," Rory said. "Look who's back-talking me now." She pushed her nose in Donnie's face, then stepped away. Rory tilted her head to the side as she studied Donnie's blouse. "Here's the deal. I do like that shirt, and it'd look real nice with the pink pants I'm wearing to the dance. So off with it, Donnie-girl. Hand it over."

"No!" The word ripped loose from a place deep inside me. How dare Rory order Donnie to take off her shirt. Donnie, who looked out for my safety. A hot wave of hatred moved through me. "Don't give it to her."

"Ah, so Amy can talk after all. Well, la-de-da. Listen to that. Amy's giving orders now." Rory turned to me, her face flushed. "And just who do you think you are, telling Donnie not to listen to me?"

"I'm sorry, Rory," Donnie said. Why was she apologizing? Was Donnie afraid for herself, or for me? "And Amy's sorry too. So you want my shirt? No problem. I'll lend it to you. Just leave us alone."

"I'll tell you what," Rory said as she paced the length of the cabin. Back and forth, then back again while Donnie and I retreated to our beds. Fear returned, yanking my heart to my throat. How stupid to have challenged Rory. What would she do to us now?

Rory glared at me when she finally spoke. "Time for a little deal here, I say. First we see what Amy's gonna wear, and then I choose: Donnie's blouse or Amy's outfit. One of you gets to keep your clothes, and one of you gives them to me. Though I can't figure out why I'm being so nice, punishing only one of you. But hey, I'm a nice person. So let's see it, Amy. Time for that little fashion show."

"Listen," Donnie said. "I'd be happy to lend you my blouse. You said it'd be perfect with your pants." She started to unbutton.

"Hold it right there. The deal is, I choose. So first I have to see what Amy's planning to wear."

Donnie still tried to rescue me. "But why not—"

"Jesus H. Christ! Don't you understand plain English? So come on now, Amy Becker. Let's have a look."

Donnie caught my eye and shrugged.

"I'm not sure what I'm wearing." My voice came slow and measured. "I haven't decided yet."

"Oh, is that so? Well then, Jess and I will help you decide. So let's see the choices." Rory walked toward me. She drew in close. "Shove off," she ordered, then sprawled across my bed as if she owned it. "And don't just stand there. Get your clothes from your trunk. We're ready to choose an outfit for you—or for me, if you catch my drift."

I stood frozen at the foot of my bed.

"Tell her the truth," Donnie said.

"The truth?" Rory smirked. "That's a good one. Your friend here's a freakin' liar. You should know that by now, Donnie-girl." Rory put her hands behind her head and sunk into my pillow, pulling muddy sneakers onto my blanket. "See, lie number one: Amy said she met Andy and Jed before the initiation. And number two: Amy told me tennis was just all right. But I know she roped Andy into being her partner, even though he wanted to play with Marcy. So tell me, Donnie-girl, why in the hell should I believe Amy now?"

"Because now she's telling the truth."

Donnie's effort to save me made Rory sit up. "Yeah, right. Like I just might believe that. So go on, Amy Becker. Show us what you've got."

I had to tell Rory the truth. "I don't have anything to wear."

"Didya hear that, Jess? My oh my. Nothing to wear, and the social's the day after tomorrow. Why don't I believe that, Amy Becker? Why do I think that maybe that package you got was filled with clothes after all?" Rory leaped off my bed and pushed me back to the window screen on the other side of the cabin. Her breath was hot in my face. "So are you gonna show us what your parents sent, or do I have to find it myself?"

If I pulled out the dress and shoes, Rory would make me the laughingstock of senior camp. My gang might come to my defense, but they wouldn't be able to stop all the giggling.

I poked at the truth. "Really. I don't have an outfit."

Rory turned toward Jessica. "Looks like it's time for a little scavenger hunt then." She pulled her sidekick to my trunk, then ordered Jessica to open the lid, revealing the top card-board tray. "Well, lookie here." Rory fingered my socks, bras, and panties—folded and stacked as if in a dresser. "Why, little Miss Prissy must think we're in some kind of fancy hotel or something." Rory faced me and chuckled. "So let me show you how we live at camp, Amy Becker. Jess, take an end."

In an instant, they lifted the tray and flipped it to the floor. Socks, balled in pairs, tumbled with my underwear. Rory trampled the pile. "You're a riot, Rory," Jessica said.

"Then why aren't Donnie and Amy laughing?" Rory marched on my panties. "Where's your sense of humor, girls?"

"It's not funny," Donnie told her.

"Oh, is that so? Well then, how's this for funny?" Rory hurled a pair of socks at Donnie's face. "You shut your trap or your trunk's next."

Donnie didn't look at me then. Somehow we both knew eye contact would make us even more ashamed. So we didn't look at each other, and we didn't say another word until Rory tossed every item from my trunk onto a heap on the floor.

She nearly choked with laughter when she uncovered the red dress. She held it up to Jessica. "Lookie here, Jess. How'd you like to wear this getup to the social? And she's even got shoes to go with it." Rory pitched my party shoes to the front of the cabin. "Now where do you suppose Little Miss Amy thought she'd be going all dressed up and fancified? Is this what you're planning to wear to the social, Amy Becker?"

"No." I said the word, but I wasn't sure Rory heard.

"Excuse me, Miss Fancy Pants. Or should I say Miss Fancy Dress? I asked you a question."

"No," I said louder.

"See," Donnie added in a last-ditch effort to save face, to save me. "She told you the truth. She doesn't have anything to wear."

"Are you just about finished?" Rory asked. She laughed as she fiddled with a strap on one of my bras, then twirled my panties on her index finger. "'Cause I've got two things to say to you, Donnie-girl. One: I'll take that blouse of yours now. So hand it over. At least one of us will be set for the social. And two: As soon as you give it to me, you'd better leave. Amy and I have unfinished business, and I won't have you standing around, getting in my way."

I prayed for someone to come in then. Anyone. Even Patsy. Or Fran and Karen, who were visiting in Bunk 8. Rory couldn't have been clearer. She was out to hurt me, and no one but Jessica would see it happen.

Donnie changed her shirt, then held out her blouse to Rory.

"Now get outta here," Rory demanded. She snatched Donnie's top with her fingertips, as if the blouse had cooties.

Donnie eyeballed her and grinned. It was then I knew what Donnie would do. She would find someone else to rescue me.

"Now, Amy Becker," Rory said as soon as the door closed behind Donnie, "time for that little chat." She plopped herself on my mountain of clothing. "You lied to me again, about the outfit, I mean. About what was in your package. See, I keep telling you I'm not stupid. Sheets and towels, you said. But all your things are right here." Rory pointed to my belongings, flowing around her. "And guess what? No new sheets. So I'm thinking what they sent you was this dress." She scrunched the red fabric and hurled it toward me. "And while I'm thinking about how to punish you for lying again, you're gonna put all your things away before anyone sees how messy you are."

I walked slowly to my trunk.

"And I'm just gonna sit right here," Rory kept on, "while you pull your clothes out from under me. So get started, girl. We haven't got all day."

I stooped to gather socks as the cabin door opened. "Hey, Ame," Erin called. I didn't look up, couldn't risk the tears. "I finally got that letter off to my folks, so I thought I'd come visit."

"Well, freckle-face, you'll just have to come back another time," Rory said. "Amy's got some straightening up to do."

"No problem. I'll help." Erin pulled a pair of shorts from under Rory's bottom. "Come on, Amy," Erin said. "We'll have this done in a jiff, especially if Rory moves her fat ass. Or the other choice is, we can send someone to find Nancy, and she can move Rory's ass. Either way, we'll have this straightened up in no time."

Rory stayed where she was, stretching her arms to guard my clothes. "This doesn't concern you, Erin. So I suggest you leave."

"Oh yes it does. Amy's my friend, and friends help each other. But of course you wouldn't know that, Rory, seeing as you don't have any real friends."

I wanted to applaud, but I didn't. I almost laughed, but laughter would have made me cry. I simply picked up another pair of socks instead.

"Oh, and one more thing, Rory," Erin said as she lifted a Takawanda shirt from under Rory's leg. "You might want to start getting your own things packed, 'cause when we tell Mr. Becker what you did, he'll probably send you home."

Without a word, Rory left the cabin, stopping only at her cubby to pull a pack of Salems from behind a stationery box. She didn't look back, not even when Jessica called, "Hey, wait for me!"

I knew Uncle Ed wouldn't kick Rory out for emptying my trunk. He would have to catch her in a "false move" himself. The only hope was our plan, which had even less of a chance now that we had started to fight back. But as Erin and I gathered my belongings, I didn't think about that. I just looked at Erin and smiled.

Chapter 11

Indecent Behavior

It didn't take long for all the seniors to find out what had happened. Once Rory thought about it, she must have figured she wouldn't be sent home for something as silly as emptying my trunk. So she didn't stop chuckling about how she had threatened to take my outfit, then found that all I had was the stupid "belle of the ball" getup my mother wanted me to wear. Everyone saw Rory doubled over on the volleyball court, laughing about my red dress and party shoes.

"I hear Aunt Sonia sent quite an outfit for the dance," Robin snickered when we met by the clothesline between our cabins. "Where does she think you're going? To the Waldorf?"

I grabbed my bathing suit.

"Regular clothes aren't good enough for you, cuz? Well, I'll tell you this: Your mother may think she's a hotshot beauty queen, but she doesn't know squat about fashion."

It was all right for me to think that about my mother, but Robin's saying it made my fists clench. Who was she to criticize how my mother dressed when her own mother squeezed herself into skintight Bermudas and nearly busted the seams of her shirts? "At least my mother's clothes fit," I mumbled as I headed toward the cabin.

The door slammed behind me.

"Your mother doesn't know squat about anything," Robin called from outside. "Jeez! She doesn't even know how to raise kids. Just look at your screwy brother."

Charlie. I no longer thought about him getting off the minibus every afternoon while I changed into my bathing suit. When had he slipped from my consciousness?

•

The day after Rory emptied my trunk, Nancy stopped Erin and me after lunch. "Come see me before the end of rest hour. I need to talk to you. Both of you."

"We have to tell her," Erin said as we walked toward Nancy's cabin.

"No we don't. She already knows."

"Whaddaya mean?"

"I could tell by her voice. She knows there's been trouble. Everyone knows."

Nancy threw the question at us the moment we opened her door. "So why didn't you tell me you had another problem with Rory?" She stood by the sink as we settled on her bed.

"Not to worry, Nance," Erin said. "It wasn't so bad. We're fine."

"That's not the point. The point is Rory can't be allowed to hurt Amy, to hurt anyone. You should have called for a counselor. You should have told Patsy. You should have told me."

"But—"

"No buts, Erin. Now I want to hear from Amy. Why didn't you tell me there'd been trouble?"

"I couldn't tell you, 'cause if I did, you would have talked to Rory or punished her or something. And I was scared that would make things worse because then she'd try to get even with me for telling." The rest I kept to myself. Telling would have gotten Rory in trouble—not enough to get her sent home, but maybe enough to ban her from the social. Telling might have ruined our plan. And even though I wasn't sure *Lion* would work, it was all we had, and I was glad we were going ahead with it.

Nancy said she had no choice now. I couldn't look at her when she told us she would have Patsy stay around the cabin during rest hour. Rory would blame this on me. I was sure of it. She'd believe I had told someone about the trunk. And Patsy would blame me too. There'd be no more time off after lunch. No more time for herself.

"You know, Amy," Nancy said, "if you want to keep playing on the edge of a volcano, that's your business. But remember: If you don't call for help before the lava flows, it might be too late."

●

Erin outfitted me for the social in madras Bermudas and a pale blue blouse. As she and Donnie fussed over which top worked better—pale blue or navy—I realized Rory had been right about one thing: What I wore didn't matter. I wouldn't have a good time no matter what. No matter how many boys might ask me to dance, no matter which girls might stay with me on the sidelines. I'd be looking over my shoulder until we'd say "Lion." I'd be waiting for Rory to trip me on the dance floor or pour bug juice on my head. I'd be checking over that same shoulder on which my mother would be sitting, criticizing my outfit and telling me I'd be dancing more if only I had worn the dress.

"So we're down to the wire, Ame," Erin said, "and I think the light blue's better on you."

"Definitely the light blue," Donnie said.

"That's fine. Really good." I pretended to care. "Thanks, you two. I don't know what I'd do without you."

"Well, good thing you won't have to find out." Erin lowered her voice to a whisper, though no one else was in Bunk 10. Rory's group had decided to do manicures in my cabin, where Patsy probably hovered over them. And Paula was off somewhere with Fran and Karen. "The only one we'll be without is Rory," Erin went on. "I still think ol' *Lion's* gonna work."

●

We gathered in The Lodge before the boys got there. My gang devoid of makeup. No black-ringed eyes, no goopy lashes. Our sole concession, Pink Pearl lipstick, the trademark of our tribe. Paula had passed it around when we dressed in Bunk 10.

Rory's band flaunted poufed hair and polished nails. War paint on their faces: powder, blush, mascara, eye shadow. Markings of the enemy.

We faced each other from opposite sides of the fire-place while younger seniors milled around the room, dodging folding chairs that lined the walls as if Reserved for Wallflower were written on them. Mr. Moose stared down on the space where the bear rug used to be.

"Well, lookie here," Rory said, revving up for battle. "No red dress, Amy?"

The moose eyes seemed to shift, finding mine, challenging me to speak. I looked down, avoiding Rory's stare, avoiding Mr. Moose.

"I'm talking to you, Amy Becker. Where did you dig up that faggy little outfit?"

I searched for Patsy. I wanted her to intercede. She had to be in The Lodge. She had walked us there.

"Y'all are mighty quiet," Patsy had said to Erin and me on the path from senior camp. "Anxious about the dance, I suppose. But there's nothin' to be nervous about. Why, you two look so nice I'll bet those Saginaw boys just won't get enough o' you gals."

We hadn't admitted we were nervous, not even to each other. But I knew we both were—our jitters having little to do with the Saginaw campers and everything to do with Rory.

"I asked where you got that faggy outfit," she said again. From the corner of my eye, I caught Andy and Jed coming into The Lodge. Andy gave me a private wave, I thought, his hand not much higher than his hip.

"Amy's outfit?" Erin answered for me as I watched the boys head toward Aunt Helen at the refreshment table. "I lent it to her."

Rory looked me up and down, then studied Erin and barked a laugh. "Guess I could've figured that out."

"Well, at least she didn't wear the dress her mother sent," Robin added, setting off giggles that snaked through her group. My stomach tossed around the meatballs I still tasted from dinner.

"Wouldn't have mattered if Amy wore that dress," Rory said once her gang settled down. "No one's gonna dance with her anyhow."

The Saginaw bus silenced them for a moment as it coughed its way to the back of The Lodge. Rory pulled Jessica by the arm. "They're finally here. Come on, Jess."

Aunt Helen darted from behind the refreshment table, where she had readied plates of cookies and pitchers of bug juice for Andy and Jed to serve. "You wait right where you are, dear," Aunt Helen said to Rory, then glanced at the rest of us as if she just noticed we were there. "Honest to goodness, don't you all look nice. Very nice, Robin honey." Robin jerked back when Aunt Helen reached to fluff her hair.

"You have to excuse my mother," my cousin announced as my aunt moved away. "She's such an idiot. I hate her."

It amazed me that Robin could say that aloud. Think it, yes. Didn't I think how I hated my mother when she told me to fix my hair, when she warned Charlie not to spill his milk, when she gave my father "the look"? But I never said it to anyone.

"Robin, have you seen your father?" Aunt Helen called now from the doorway of The Lodge.

None of us had seen Uncle Ed. Other than Aunt Helen, the only adults in the room were the counselors from Bunks 7, 8, and 10. They huddled by the piano as if ready for a sing-along. Nancy had said she would stop by, but the boys arrived before she did.

We stiffened—even Rory and Jessica, I noticed—at the sound of male voices as the Saginaw campers walked toward the front of The Lodge. Then heavy footsteps on the porch. Hearty laughter.

I sang to myself to steady my nerves and to drown out my mother, who had taken up residence in my head again. *I told you to wear the dress, Amy.* What came without thinking was the song we'd been singing in the dining hall since the first day of camp:

> *The boys at our socials will never be*
> *Tall, dark, and handsome and six-foot-three.*
> *The boys we call our own*
> *Will wear glasses and braces and smell of cologne.*

"Welcome. Welcome." Aunt Helen greeted them with a chuckle. "Come on in."

The boys clumped in groups as we did. They glanced around trying not to be obvious, taking in the room and the girls. Aunt Helen chatted with a couple of Saginaw counselors. She scanned The Lodge as she talked, looking for her absent husband, no doubt.

But then the music started, and I lost sight of her. Jed placed a 45 on the record player set up on a table by the refreshment area. As Bobby Lewis sang "Tossin' and Turnin' All Night," boys broke from their friends to choose partners. I looked down as they checked us out.

Everyone backed up to make space in the middle of the room. Robin was the first to be chosen. She danced with one of the few boys who negated our song about socials. Even Aunt Helen noticed Robin's catch. My aunt stopped flitting around and beamed at her daughter, joined now in the center of The Lodge by assorted seniors from every cabin. Soon half the campers were bopping around.

I didn't see Rory in the mix of dancers. "Probably dragged Jessica outside for a cigarette when nobody asked them to dance," Erin said. "Maybe your uncle will catch them smoking and kick her out for that. All our planning, and she'll get herself in trouble before we put ol' *Lion* to the test. Wouldn't that be something?"

Andy smiled at me when Erin and I walked toward the refreshment area, where younger seniors gathered.

"Hey, Amy," Andy called over the "Itsy Bitsy Teenie Weenie Yellow Polka Dot Bikini" song. "I was hoping I'd be the first to ask you to dance."

"Mr. B-Becker won't l-l-like that." Jed focused on a stack of 45s.

"But I don't see him anywhere," Andy said. "So put a record on and cover for me, okay?"

My heart pumped fast. I looked at Erin, eager for permission to leave her.

She smiled. "Go ahead, Ame."

Andy clapped Jed on the back. "See if you can find the Big Bopper."

Girls raised eyebrows as Andy came around from behind the table. He grabbed my hand and led me to the center of the room. The record started.

"Good. He got it. You ready, Amy?"

I couldn't find words—not even a simple yes. Heat pulsed through me as our bodies moved in step to the music, in step with each other. Andy sang along to "Chantilly Lace." He looked at me as he sang and we danced and the room spun around.

I didn't see Rory work her way toward us. I didn't notice Uncle Ed as he entered The Lodge, Patsy not far behind, as I would hear later.

"I told you nobody'd dance with you." Rory's words broke the spell. "Not a real boy anyhow. Just a pot-scrubbing twerp."

"Well, I don't see *you* dancing with *any* boy, Rory," Andy hurled back. We kept moving, but in half-time now, our spirits zapped.

"It's okay, Andy," I lied, eager to keep the lion caged. And then it hit me, right on the Bopper's last words. Andy was right. Rory wasn't dancing at all. Our plan couldn't work if she didn't find a boy.

I had to talk to Erin, who came from one direction while Uncle Ed elbowed his way across the room from the other. "I don't pay you to socialize with my campers, young man."

The room quieted, even though Jed had put on another record. Andy's eyes caught mine, then lowered in embarrassment. "I'm sorry, sir. I didn't think you'd mind."

Rory grinned as if she'd just won a contest—which she had, in a sense. Instead of us getting her in trouble, she had drawn Uncle Ed's attention to me. And in that instant, when Andy stalked back to the refreshment table and Rory's smile grew wider, something inside me snapped.

"We have to get her, and I don't care what her father does," I told Erin as we walked to the folding chairs. "We've got to get her with a boy, and fast."

Erin raised her voice over Del Shannon's "Runaway." "Not to worry," she said, patting my leg before she got up and scouted the room. I watched her stride across the floor, head high, shoulders back. Whatever Erin was about to do, she was sure it would work.

She talked to two boys, then pointed to Rory and Jessica. One of the boys laughed as if Erin had just told the funniest joke. The other didn't look as if he found it amusing, but he smiled just the same. The laughing boy put a hand on Erin's shoulder and reclaimed his composure. As he and his friend zoomed in on Rory and Jessica, Erin headed back to me.

"Mission accomplished," she declared, "and I couldn't have asked for a better song."

The boy who'd been laughing pressed Rory tight as Connie Francis sang "Where The Boys Are." The other one danced with Jessica.

"Now all we have to do is tell Jed we need more slow songs," Erin said. "And then we say the word."

Andy avoided my eyes as he handed me a cup of bug juice. "Sorry, Amy." He shook his head. "I wish I could've kept dancing with you."

Jed told Erin he had lots of slow songs. "B-but Mr. B-Becker might not want too m-m-many slow ones."

"Yeah, but I don't see him. So come on, Jed. A favor for a friend." Erin put my bug juice on the table. She pulled me away before I could think of anything to say to Andy. "Time to get in position," she said.

We rounded everyone up. We didn't say "lion," though. We simply said it was time. The code word would have made this a game, and now we were certain it wasn't.

Rory walked right past the lineup by the door, not stopping to question, not pausing to gloat. As her new boyfriend hustled her outside, she didn't even look back to see if adults were watching. Maybe she knew she didn't have to worry: Takawanda counselors danced with their Saginaw counterparts; Patsy and Uncle Ed seemed to have vanished; and Aunt Helen hurried back and forth from the kitchen, replenishing cookies and carrying pitchers of bug juice.

"We'll give them a few minutes to get hot and heavy out there," Erin reminded me, "and then we nail 'em." She pulled me over to Donnie. "I think he'll keep her busy for a while," she told our gatekeeper, "but if they want to come in, don't let 'em."

Erin turned to me. "Now we find your uncle, which shouldn't be hard. I saw him talking to your aunt right after he chewed Andy out. Maybe said he wasn't feeling well or something, 'cause he went upstairs. So this is it. Let's get him."

Erin and I skulked up the steps. She pushed me to my knees at the top rung. "Stay low in case anyone looks up here. We'll try one room at a time. And when we find your uncle, you tell him there's a problem and you need him to come outside right away."

Two empty bedrooms and a bathroom. The fourth door was closed. "I'm opening it," Erin whispered.

"You can't just barge in."

"Do you want to be polite, or do you want to get Rory?"

"Get Rory," I answered, knowing that politeness didn't count anymore. The only thing that mattered was Uncle Ed's catching Rory in her final false move.

Erin reached up to turn the knob, then shoved the door open. She pushed me into the room, where Patsy sat at the edge of the bed. Uncle Ed stood facing her, very close, his back to us. He whirled around, hand on his zipper.

I couldn't talk. I couldn't move. Erin yanked me from the room.

We ran downstairs, hunched over so no one would see us. "Get your aunt," Erin ordered.

"Oh my God. No."

"Just so she can catch Rory," Erin explained.

I looked around at the dancing, the campers, the Saginaw boys—all hazy and unfamiliar. "I don't see Aunt Helen," I told Erin.

"Try the kitchen. Say anything to get her outside. And hurry. I'll meet you by the door."

I babbled something about noises when I pulled my aunt away from the refrigerator. We raced across The Lodge, parting dancers as we pushed through. Erin followed us out.

What greeted me made my breath catch. It wasn't just Rory and her new boyfriend, but Robin and a boy too. The guys explored the girls' breasts while the girls simply tilted their heads back, eyes closed.

Aunt Helen grabbed Robin's arm. "What in the devil's gotten into you, Robin? You should be ashamed of yourself!" She pried Robin from the Saginaw camper who gave her up without argument. "Just wait till I tell your father about this." She dragged Robin to the porch steps, ignoring the boy who had massaged her daughter's chest, disregarding Rory and her beau.

Robin chuckled. "Yeah. Go ahead and tell Dad, if you can find him."

Aunt Helen pulled her toward the door. "For your information, he's upstairs resting."

"Right, Mom. Believe what you want. What do I care?"

Rory smirked at Erin and me. We watched her guide her boyfriend toward the side of The Lodge, away from view.

Erin steered me inside. Our gang blitzed us with questions. I let Erin explain how Uncle Ed was upstairs, and how Aunt Helen hadn't even noticed Rory. "And for this I gave up the boy of my dreams," Paula said. "Nice work, Erin. We still have Rory, and now I don't have a boy to dance with."

We still have Rory. Those words pounded in my brain with images of Patsy and Uncle Ed upstairs; Rory grinning at Erin and me.

"Look it, you guys," Erin said as we huddled with our group. "We'll find a way. We'll make another plan. But there's nothing else we can do tonight. So let's just enjoy the rest of the social."

Paula and Karen hustled to find the boys they had left for guard duty. Donnie and Fran headed for refreshments.

"Not to worry, Ame," Erin said. "If things get really bad, we'll tell your uncle he has to send Rory home or we'll spill his little secret."

Confusion and anger pressed like bricks on my chest. "No," I told Erin. "I can't blackmail my own uncle. And I don't want you to tell anyone either."

"Okay, I hear you. We'll just come up with another plan then." Erin spoke as Chubby Checker sang "The Twist."

"But right now, Ame," Erin continued, "let's dance."

I couldn't believe she went on as if nothing had happened. Just thinking about what Uncle Ed and Patsy must have been doing made me want to throw up.

Erin swiveled her hips to draw two boys. "Yes, we'd love to dance," she said, before the Saginaw campers even asked.

I didn't notice Uncle Ed come downstairs. I didn't see him come over to me. "You stop that gyrating this instant, young lady, or I'll call your father and tell him about this indecent behavior."

I couldn't look at him, though I knew I had more to tell than he did. I turned from my partner before the tears came.

Uncle Ed followed me to the wall of chairs. "And don't you ever tell anyone what you saw upstairs. 'Cause if anyone ever hears about it—and I mean *anyone*—you're in big trouble." Then he walked away, leaving me alone.

Erin found me on the sidelines. "Uncle Ed's really mad," I told her. "He said he'd call my father if I kept twisting."

"So let him. I'll bet your father would be happy to hear you were dancing. Isn't that what you're supposed to do at a social?"

"He said I was being indecent." Tears finally broke through.

Erin put a hand on my back. "Come on. He's just trying to scare you so you don't snitch on him. I mean, who's the indecent one here?"

I didn't know how long Patsy had been watching us, but once I started crying, I suppose she felt safe coming over. "I just want to say nothing happened upstairs. I mean I just went up to find a bathroom, and Mr. Becker was up there. So we were just havin' a little chat, that's all."

"Yeah, sure," Erin said, pulling me off my chair. I sideswiped Patsy as The Tokens started singing "The Lion Sleeps Tonight."

Donnie, Paula, Fran, and Karen giggled as they wandered over. When Nancy finally arrived, she found us huddled in the corner, everyone singing but Erin and me.

"I thought you'd all be dancing," Nancy said. "But it looks like you're having a great time together. And that's what camp's about: fun and friendship."

She forgot the third part: secrets. But I didn't need a reminder about that.

Chapter 12

It's Our Secret

The night of the Saginaw social, I dreamed of a white door. I stand on tiptoe and, with little-girl fingers, grab the old-fashioned glass doorknob. Locked. I push, try again. A whisper. A moan behind the door. Who's there? I squeeze the knob. Turn harder. Still locked. Locked out. Always the same, this dream that came again and again.

I stirred in my camp bed. In the haze between sleep and awakening, the door filled my mind. I drifted back to sleep, back to a time before Charlie—a time before we had a house, when my parents and I lived in an apartment. My father's at night school. I try not to bother my mother. She vacuums the living room while I sit in the big chair where Dad reads to me on weekends. In his absence, I trace with my index finger illustrations in *The Tall Book of Fairy Tales*: Cinderella, Rumpelstiltskin, Hansel and Gretel. I tell the stories, voice hushed so my mother won't get angry. She fluffs the cushions on the sofa. "Remember the rules, Amy. Don't tell your father I had company today."

The doorbell rings. "It's our secret," my mother warns. She sends me to my room, across from my parents'. "And if you come out before I tell you, you'll be punished."

I curl up with Puppy, my stuffed animal, and listen for noises. Footsteps in the hallway. Then whispering. The floor creaks by our bedrooms.

I open my book to the picture of a gingerbread house. My father's squeaky voice plays in my head:

> Nibble, nibble like a mouse.
> Who is nibbling at my house?

"Stupid goose!" cries the witch when Gretel refuses to poke in the oven to see if it's hot. So the witch shows her how. Gretel pushes her all the way in, slams the oven door, and runs to save her brother.

I finish the story and squirm, the urge to pee so strong I clamp my legs. My mother will punish me if I leave my room. Yet I have to go so badly that I'll wet my pants if I wait. And the one time I did that, she got really angry. "Big girls don't make sissy in their clothes, Amy."

I sneak out and hear my mother moan. Is someone hurting her? I stand by my parents' door and listen to my mother whimper, then something that sounds like a slap. "No," she whispers. "Oh, no. No more."

Urine runs down my leg. I have to save my mother, chase that bad visitor away. I reach for the glass knob. But then I hear my mother cry out, "Yes. Oh yes!"

Is she hurt or is she happy? If the visitor is hurting her, I have to help. If I don't, she'll be mad. She'll say I should have heard her calling. She'll say I should know when to break the rules. And if she's happy, she won't be angry with me for breaking them.

I stand in a puddle of pee. My mother speaks again as I grab the doorknob. "We can't keep doing this. What if Lou finds out? Or Helen?"

I put my ear to the door.

"I can't stop, Sonia," the visitor says in a voice I recognize. "I need you."

I unglue myself from the floor and fly into the bathroom. "Jesus Christ!" I hear Uncle Ed say. Has he stepped in my puddle? I stiffen behind the closed bathroom door. "Could Amy have heard us?"

"Of course not," my mother answers. "She just waited too long to use the toilet."

Footsteps—away from me now. I keep my ear to the bathroom door until my mother comes back. She flings a pair of underpants at me. "Well, don't just stand there, Amy. Clean yourself up."

Words sit like pebbles in my throat. *I'm sorry. I won't tell.*

I put on dry panties as I hear my mother mopping the floor. Disinfectant dizzies me when I step into the hallway.

"Now go to your room for wetting your pants like a baby," my mother says. "And if you ever tell anyone I had a visitor, you will stay in your room for a day."

●

I awoke in my Takawanda bed. The dream turned in my mind. So many details. Too vivid. Too real. And that's when

133

I knew: It wasn't a dream, but a memory that had surfaced while I slept.

I couldn't stop thinking about it. Uncle Ed and my mother. And my father? "Brothers support each other," he had told her. A sour taste filled my mouth as I searched the past. Like Hansel, I needed bread crumbs to guide me. How often had Uncle Ed visited? And when had my mother started hating him? Clearly she did now, telling my father she didn't care what Ed said about anything.

I couldn't stop thinking about Uncle Ed and Patsy too. How could she sit next to me at breakfast and pretend nothing had happened?

"Why so quiet this morning?" she asked, calling for conversation, which didn't come. "I guess you gals are still plumb worn out from all that dancin' ya did."

A grin crept up Rory's face as she picked the grapes from her dish of canned fruit salad. "Well now, how would you know about our dancing? Seems to me you weren't around much last night, Patsy."

I jerked in my seat. Had Rory forgotten Uncle Ed's warning about inappropriate behavior, or had her conquest at the social fueled her courage?

Patsy's spoon hit the table. "Just what are you sayin', Rory?"

"Seems clear to me." Rory glared at Patsy as if daring her to stare back. "Yes indeedy. The more I think about it, the more it seems you and old Mr. Becker must have taken off before the boys even got there, 'cause I sure don't remember seeing either of you around much." She jabbed Jessica's shoulder. "Am I right or am I right?"

I lowered my head, afraid to lock eyes with Rory and afraid to meet Patsy's. If she thought I had snitched, Patsy would tell Uncle Ed. And he would find something awful about me to tell my father. Something much worse than twisting.

"And just where do you think I was?" Patsy asked.

The table stilled.

"We all know where you were," Rory answered. "Don't we girls?"

I felt Patsy looking at me. What should I do? If I said I didn't know where Patsy had been, Rory would go crazy. But if I played along with Rory, Patsy would be angry. Fruit salad syrup clogged my throat. I ran for the bathroom.

●

By that afternoon Rory had already guessed what we'd tried to do. "I keep telling you I'm not stupid, Amy Becker," she whispered after lunch. "I'm thinking there must've been some reason you dragged your aunt outside last night. What I'm thinking is you wanted to get me in trouble."

Patsy stayed with us all rest hour, playing counselor to the fullest, keeping Rory in check and checking our letters.

Dear Charlie,

Camp is great! We had our first social. It was so much fun. The boys were really nice, and I danced all night.

By the way, Dad should definitely bring his tennis racquet when you come to visit. I've been playing a lot, and I won my first tournament match. And you should bring a bathing suit. The lake is really beautiful. I love swimming in it. On visiting day, we can swim together.

Well, I gotta scoot, scoot, skedaddle. I love you, buddy, and I miss you so much.

Love,
Amy

I covered the words when Patsy put a hand on my back. I didn't want her to read my lies—though she certainly had told enough of her own, pretending to be my friend, telling me Uncle Ed's "a mighty fine man." Now her touch made me squirm.

"When you gals finish your letters," Patsy said, squeezing my shoulder, "y'all go on out if you want. But I'll stay around for a while, in case any o' you feel like talkin' or anything."

My private invitation to chat, I assumed. She probably wanted to make sure Erin and I hadn't told her secret: Patsy and Uncle Ed, right there in The Lodge with the seniors and Aunt Helen downstairs.

But what I thought about even more was my mother and Uncle Ed, right there in my parents' room with me across the hall. Uncle Ed could threaten to tell my father about my twisting, but I knew then he wouldn't. He had to keep me on his good side. I shared my uncle's secrets, and his lies outweighed mine.

I wriggled from Patsy's grip and tossed my sealed letter on her bed. Without a word, I left the cabin.

●

How would I act toward my mother on visiting day? My memory of her and Uncle Ed ruined whatever chance we still had at a good relationship. I wondered why she had cheated on my father—and with his brother, no less. My stomach turned when I thought about that.

I thought about Charlie too. I pictured him stepping off the yellow minibus, jumping into my arms.

Did Charlie know he would see me soon? Surely he'd have no concept of visiting day. "Not to worry," Erin said when I told her I wanted my brother to have fun. "Visitors get to use all the equipment and everything, even the tennis courts. And everyone gets to swim. Your brother'll have a ball."

I wanted to believe her, but I couldn't. Charlie didn't like basketball and tennis. He would want me to read him a story or build with blocks.

And what about Rory? How would she push her way into that day? If Rory had no visitors, her anger could boil over onto Charlie.

"Remember, Amy Becker," Rory told me again, "I'm not stupid. I know you tried to get me in trouble at the social. So maybe I'll get even with you on visiting day—maybe even do something to that retard brother of yours."

Dear Dad,
    I hope you get this before you leave for Maine, because I don't think Charlie should come.

He won't have fun here, and I don't want him to take such a long trip and not even enjoy himself.

Camp isn't a good place for kids. I mean, it's not a good place for visitors Charlie's age. The lake is so cold he won't want to go swimming. And with so many people here that day, we won't find a quiet place to play. So maybe Mom could stay home with him.

I don't have time to write Charlie a separate letter, and I know you can explain this to him better than I can. Please tell him I love him so much, and I can't wait to see him at the end of the summer. I'll try to write to him tomorrow.

Love,
Amy

P.S. Everyone says they share the snacks their parents bring on visiting day. So please bring lots of Ring Dings and Hershey bars and Hostess cupcakes—enough for all my friends. Thanks, Dad. Can't wait to see you!

●

My father must have called Uncle Ed with my letter still in hand. Nancy smiled when she said my uncle asked to see me after breakfast—a smile that said *Don't worry. I'll be there.*

She lingered at the owner's table even after Aunt Helen had given up on the pancakes. "Go on now, Nancy," Uncle Ed said. "I'm sure you have plenty to do for tomorrow's visiting schedule."

"But if there's a problem, perhaps I could help."

"No. No problem at all. Just a little family matter. No need for you to waste your time."

My stomach told me I should have skipped breakfast. I couldn't look at Uncle Ed.

"So, Amy," Uncle Ed said once Nancy left. "Why did you tell your father camp's not a good place?"

I felt my uncle's eyes on me. "I didn't," I said to my lap.

"Don't lie to me. I know exactly what you said. You of all people. How could you tell your father not to bring Charlie?"

"But that's not—"

"I'm not finished, young lady. And look at me when I talk to you."

My head felt like a bowling ball as I tried to focus on the pine wall behind my uncle.

"Now I know you don't have many friends here, though your father seems to think you have plenty. And if that makes him happy, let him think what he wants. Our little secret." He winked, then went on. "I'm sure it's hard, trying to be popular like my Robin. And it must be embarrassing to have a brother like Charlie. But to say your mother should stay home with him? Well, that's just mean and selfish."

"But I was only looking out for Charlie." I had to speak up, say more, tell Uncle Ed what Rory had said. Then he might ask Patsy—or Nancy even—to keep a closer eye on her tomorrow. Or maybe he would think Rory's threat against Charlie bad enough to send her home.

"Looking out for Charlie, my eye," Uncle Ed said.

"No, really, Uncle Ed. Rory says she'll hurt him. That's why I don't want him to come."

My uncle took a long drink of coffee. "So let me get this straight. Rory says she'll hurt your brother tomorrow?"

I pushed out a "Yes" so weak I didn't know if I said it aloud.

"And why would Rory want to hurt Charlie?"

I didn't know how to tell Uncle Ed about this war that had started before we'd even gotten to camp. Yet I had to protect Charlie, who would be here, for sure, the next day.

I made myself look at my uncle then, stared him right in the eye without cringing. "Because Rory hates me, and she knows I love Charlie."

"Hate's a pretty strong word, young lady."

"But Rory's been mean to me since the beginning of camp. I'm scared she'll do something to Charlie."

"Come on, Amy. A retarded eight-year-old? Why would she pick on him?"

"I told you," I said, lowering my head. "She's mean and she hates me and she's always looking for trouble. I just don't want Charlie to get hurt."

"Well, trust me on this: I run a great camp, and no one gets hurt here. Nancy and Patsy tell me everything that goes on. And my Robin does too. So I know there's been trouble. But from what Robin says, you bring it on yourself. You and your little friend Erin, you're different from the other girls. You don't fit in.

"Now, Amy, I'm not saying Rory doesn't have problems, but Robin says she's not a bad kid. So I'm willing to give her the benefit of the doubt now. And I'm assuming there won't be any trouble tomorrow.

"So let's forget the past—*everything* that happened—and just have a great visiting day."

Though I didn't look up, I was sure Uncle Ed must have winked again.

"Your parents are entitled to some happiness." He pushed his chair from the table. "Don't deny them the pleasure of seeing you cheerful for a change. They've always wanted you to be popular like Robin. They worry so much about you and Charlie. So let's not give them anything else to worry about."

Later I would think about whether that was true. Did both my parents worry about me? My father did, I knew—always wanting me to be happy. But my mother? All she wanted was for me to be perfect, like the pillows on her sofa.

Uncle Ed continued as he stood. "Now go back to your cabin and help with cleanup. I expect this place to sparkle tomorrow. And I expect you to make your parents happy I allowed them to send you here."

So Uncle Ed had *allowed* my parents to send me to Takawanda, I told myself as I left the dining hall. *Allowed* them, as if my parents had come begging to him. Why couldn't he let my father feel like the big man just once? Was it because Uncle Ed thought my father had won the marriage contest while he'd gotten the booby prize?

I walked back to senior camp with shoulders so heavy I could barely support them.

Chapter 13

Scrawnier than a Month Ago

Takawanda buzzed on visiting day morning. "I'm so excited," Erin said after breakfast. "Whaddaya think your parents'll bring?"

I wanted to share her enthusiasm. But if Rory decided to get Charlie, she would figure a way to do it. And not only that, but a whole day with my mother. How could I act as if nothing were different than when I had left for camp?

"I asked for Ring Dings and Hershey bars and Hostess cupcakes," I said. My voice sounded as if I'd asked for spinach, broccoli, and Brussels sprouts.

"And my mom baked chocolate chip cookies and brownies." Erin glowed with glee. "We'll have a feast."

It was my turn to say something, but I didn't know what.

"Look it. Ring Dings and chocolate bars and cookies and brownies," Erin went on. "What could be bad about that?"

Still no words came as we entered senior camp. I glanced to make sure Rory wasn't behind us.

"Come on, Ame. Today's the best day of the summer. And we'll all be together at the picnic—you and your parents and Charlie and me and my folks. I can't wait!"

●

I ran into Robin at the clothesline toward the end of cleanup.

"Here's a news flash for you, cuz," she teased. "Some families bring their dogs with them."

My bathing suit fell to the ground. I hadn't thought about dogs—about Charlie and dogs.

"But don't worry," Robin kept on. "I'm sure the dogs that'll be here today are nothing but itty-bitty ones. You know, the kinds whose bark is worse than their bite. Probably couldn't even frighten a crazy scaredy-cat like your brother." Robin toed my swimsuit, coating it with dirt and pine needles, then hooked it with a stick. She shoved the grimy suit at my chest. "Better clean this before Aunt Sonia sees what a mess you made."

Robin burst into laughter, and I wondered when she had turned into Rory. I looked toward the sound of applause—Rory at the screen in my cabin. She gave a thumbs-up to Robin, who strutted into Bunk 10 as if she had just been crowned prom queen.

"What's goin' on?" I thought I heard Patsy ask. I didn't listen for Rory's answer, just shook out my bathing suit and trudged into the cabin.

Rory lounged on her bed, ignoring Patsy's "two minutes till inspection" warning while everyone else checked that they'd made theirs with proper hospital corners and that they had neatened the toiletries in their cubbies. I rolled my soiled suit in a towel and took out my other one—the flimsy tank that showed my nipples.

Erin met me outside before the bell rang. We banded with seniors milling around, not punching the tetherball, not even braiding lanyards. Jessica huddled with Rory's gang, though Rory didn't join them. Neither did Robin. She pushed past me on her way into our cabin, where she stayed with Rory while Patsy sat on the step, her back perfectly straight. She caught my eye and smiled. I looked away.

At the sound of the bell, we ran toward the rec hall to greet our parents. By the time we approached the dining hall, most of the seniors had raced ahead of us.

Erin pulled me along. "Let's go," she said. "I want to be there when they arrive."

Eagerness blinded her to my lack of excitement. Though I wanted to see my father and Charlie, I certainly didn't want to see my mother.

I freed myself from Erin's grasp. "Go ahead. I'll meet you." Then I lied without pause. "My father said they might be late."

"If you insist." Erin sprang from my side. "See you there," she called over her shoulder.

I looked over *my* shoulder to check for Rory, though I didn't think I would see her. No need for her to come to the rec hall; she had no one to meet. I passed the dining hall on my left and turned up the path, as familiar to me now as the hallways of my own house. Had it been only four weeks since my parents and Charlie dropped me off at the bus? Only a month since Rory had steamrolled over me?

The area in front of the rec hall reminded me of the sidewalk by the Museum of Natural History: another jumble of campers. But now everyone wore Takawanda uniforms. And now parents carried the bags—shopping bags stuffed with cookies, cupcakes, candy, potato chips, pretzels, and Cracker Jack, I imagined. Parents hauled goodies across the grassy field, where Andy and Jed directed cars into makeshift spots. I looked at the clearing, not so much to find our car as to catch Andy's attention. But Uncle Ed was there to welcome families. So I doubted Andy would wave, even if he wanted to.

I watched as Andy guided the brown Impala into a space. My mother got out first. She fluffed her pale green skirt, then reached into the car for a canvas bag. She looked past me toward a group of mothers in Bermudas wrapping arms around their daughters. My father stepped out next. He stretched as if he had just driven up from New York, though I knew he'd done the driving the day before. For a moment, I forgot about my mother, forgot about Rory even, as I waved for my father to notice me. But he focused on helping Charlie out of the car. Then with one hand gripping my brother, Dad stretched back into the car with his other. He pulled out a grocery bag. My goodies. A feast to share with Erin. Where was she? I realized I hadn't looked for her in the mix of campers and parents.

My father spotted me as he hefted the bag in his arm. I wanted to run over, to hug him, to hold Charlie. But Pee-Wee barricaded us—those who listened, that is—behind sawhorses.

"Amy!" my father called, his voice a kiss over the screeches of campers reuniting with parents. He placed Charlie's hand in my mother's, thrust his out in a giant hello.

"Dad! Hi!" I yelled. "Charlie!" I pushed my way around the barrier. "Charlie, over here, buddy!"

His face lit as he and my mother approached, my father at their side. Charlie wriggled to free himself, to zoom in for my hug. My mother looked up and nodded at me. I held up a hand but couldn't get it to wave to her, couldn't push out a *Hi, Mom*. "Hey, buddy!" I shouted again to my brother.

Charlie pulled loose. His hands flapped as he flew toward me. He jumped into my arms. Was he even scrawnier than a month ago?

"I'm so happy to see you, buddy. I've missed you so much."

"Amy," he whispered. Then "Amy?"—his voice rising with the question.

"I'm right here, buddy. And we've got the whole day together." I didn't try to put Charlie down when my father reached for a hug. He had placed the grocery bag, top folded over, on the ground. No packages of cupcakes spilling out. No multiple shopping bags like other parents had brought.

My mother leaned forward. I forced myself not to pull away when her lips grazed my cheek.

"You look great, honey," my father said.

My mother studied the printed visiting day schedule, which I knew would end up in that metal box in her closet. She looked at her watch. "Lou, get Charlie down. It's time to see Amy's cabin."

"All right, son." My father tried to loosen Charlie's arms. He clutched me harder. "It's okay now, son. You can hold Amy's hand. We're just going to take a walk."

"No." Charlie's voice came low but firm. Then louder and louder, until his "No!" filled the air. I tuned out the laughter, wanted to ignore the pointing and stares.

"I mean it now, son." I heard the effort in my father's voice, his trying not to lash out at Charlie.

Everyone headed toward the cabins. I looked for Erin, but I didn't see her. Instead, I saw Aunt Helen, dressed like a counselor in black Bermudas and a white, sleeveless blouse. She torpedoed toward us. "Why'd you bring him, Lou?" She nodded toward Charlie, still attached to my neck, then faced my mother. "You could have stayed home with him, Sonia. We don't want any problems today."

"Charlie won't be any trouble," my father answered. "Ed said he'd be welcome."

"Well then. In that case..." Aunt Helen's thought floated away. "And how was your trip?"

"Fine." My mother's voice banned further conversation.

"It's good to see you, Helen," my father said, kissing his sister-in-law's cheek.

"I know Ed wants to talk to you, though Lord knows it's a busy day around here. But anyhoodle, I'm sure he'll catch up with you later."

Would Uncle Ed tell my father I had trouble with the popular girls? Would my mother hear it too? Though I didn't want to care what she might think, I still did.

Charlie's fingers dug into my back as Aunt Helen left us, the last family group, alone in front of the rec hall. "Come on, buddy," I whispered. "I've got you now." Charlie loosened his arms and let me stand him on the ground. I gripped his hand. "I'll show you my cabin."

"And Mom and I want to meet all your friends." Dad sounded so happy. "You know, honey, I was worried about you when your last letter came. But Uncle Ed says it's been a great season. I'm so glad you're having such a good time."

•

We walked the deserted path to senior camp. The other campers already nestled in cabins, giggling with their families, I was sure. Sharing goodies.

My father cradled the grocery bag in his arm like a child. I held Charlie's hand. My mother followed, her white leather shoes squeaking with each step. Why couldn't she have worn sneakers like the other mothers?

"So what'd you bring?" I asked my father as I tapped the bag, lumpy and hard. No crinkle of cupcake wrappers. No stack of chocolate bars. "Did you get what I asked for?"

"What you asked for is garbage," my mother answered from behind. "And it looks like you haven't slimmed down, not even with all the activities here." I had expected my mother's negative verdict on my appearance. I just hadn't thought it would come so fast.

"Sonia, please, Sonia. Amy looks great. And the important thing is she's having fun."

"It's okay, Dad." My lies started pouring out. "It doesn't matter what you brought."

Charlie stamped on a pinecone, kicking up a cloud of dirt. "Stop it," my mother ordered. "Walk nicely."

I squeezed Charlie's hand to tell him he could walk any way he wanted. Fourteen years under my mother's thumb, then four weeks under Rory's. It had finally gotten to me.

"So how's tennis?" my father asked. "Any chance we'll get to hit? My racquet's in the car."

"I don't understand why you're playing so much tennis," my mother jumped in, her feet at our heels so she wouldn't miss a word. "You're supposed to be trying new things, making friends in different sports." How could she love me so little yet care so much about which friends I had? And what did it matter, anyhow? My friends would never win my mother's approval: not smart enough, not pretty enough, not popular enough.

I couldn't talk to her about my friends without risking a clash. And if I started something, my father might change sides. I knew that fine line between his keeping my mother from getting annoyed and his keeping me from becoming wounded. Yet that day more than ever, I needed Dad's support, his "You look great, honey," his joy at the thought I had friends.

He seemed to study me as we walked. Was my father looking for clues, a crack in my surface? I thought again about what Uncle Ed might have told him.

"From what you say, honey, you've got lots of friends. And if you can play tennis and try new things too, why there's nothing wrong with that." So my father agreed with me. I smiled, even as I felt my mother's eyes pinning me from the rear.

"Hey there, Amy." Patsy greeted us at the door to Bunk 9. I tightened my hold on Charlie as I took in the cabin: guests and food and gifts. Where was Rory? "I was wond'rin' when I'd have the pleasure of meetin' your family," Patsy said.

My father fell for the drawl that used to hold me like a hug. "Lou Becker," he announced, smiling as he extended his hand.

"Patsy Kridell. And it's right nice to meet ya, sir. Your daughter's a mighty fine gal, a pleasure to have in my cabin."

My mother stepped forward, hands at her side. "I'm Mrs. Becker. Amy's mother."

"Pleased to meet ya, ma'am." Patsy reached toward Charlie. "And you must be Amy's brother."

Charlie latched on to my leg.

"Ah, you're a shy one, are ya?" Patsy backed away, peering at Charlie as though she recognized him from somewhere, then encouraged us to make ourselves at home.

We hovered near the door as if we had crashed a private party. I wanted Donnie to invite us in, to prove I had a friend. But she stayed on her bed, laughing with her parents while she counted red licorice whips.

"So, home sweet home," my father said after a moment. "This is nice. Which is your bed?"

Two empty cots: Rory's and mine. "That last one," I answered, disengaging Charlie to take his hand.

Jessica, Fran, and Karen barely looked up as we passed. But Donnie scooted around her parents and held out a red candy string. "Hi, Charlie. Want one?" Charlie burrowed into me.

"Thanks," I answered. "I'll take it for him."

My father placed the grocery bag on my bed, where it sat unopened. Why bother? My mother had surely vetoed my list, opting for something healthy, no doubt. For an instant, I almost envied Rory—no visitors to impress, no shame over unwanted treats.

Uncle Ed had been right about the intrusion of the home world into the camp world, as his "no-phone-calls letter" stated. Parents didn't belong in this place, where all the rules were broken.

Charlie hopped up on my bed and pulled his stick legs to his chest. "No shoes on the bed. You know the rules," my mother said as she stood by my cubby, studying the arrangement of soap, shampoo, and toothpaste. I was glad I had stripped the caked-on residue from the tube earlier that morning.

"It's fine, Mom," I murmured, anxious to avoid a scene. I sat next to my brother and stroked his back. "The rules are different here. His shoes don't bother me."

"Then it's good we didn't buy that more expensive blanket." Did she notice mine was the only bed not dressed in Hudson Bay?

"Sonia, please, Sonia. You don't have to worry about Amy's things here." My father fidgeted with the nail from which my laundry bag and robe dangled. "How 'bout introducing us to your friends, honey." It wasn't a request but a directive, my father's effort to stem the tension between my mother and me.

I tried for a deep breath, but the air locked in my chest. I didn't want to hear what my mother would say when she learned I wasn't popular. And what would my father think when he found I'd been lying? I pushed out Donnie's name, had to say it twice before she heard me over chatter and the ripping open of candy wrappers. I introduced her to my parents. I could see my mother sizing her up. Donnie: pudgy thighs, untucked shirt. A low ranking on the Sonia Becker scale. "And your other friends?" she asked.

Before I could answer, Charlie opened the grocery bag and pulled out a nectarine. It plopped on the floor. I jumped to pick it up as my mother started in. "Behave now, Charlie. Don't touch anything else."

Should I put the fruit back in the bag or toss it in the garbage? I stood there, not knowing which would make my mother less angry. I turned the nectarine in my hand. The soft spot where it had hit the floor made me think of a baby's head. My father had told me about that space, where the skull isn't fused, the first time I held Charlie, when my parents brought him home from the hospital. I remembered glancing at my mother, at her tired eyes. I was only six, but I'd noticed how sad she looked.

"Don't worry, Mom," I said in my camp cabin now as I tried to protect my brother. "It's only a nectarine."

"You have no idea how much fruit costs."

"Sonia, please, Sonia. It's one nectarine."

As if my mother hadn't heard, she went on about the money she'd spent for the best fruit she could find—more than any parents spent on junk food, she repeated several times. And while I stood there fingering the bruised nectarine, Charlie toppled the grocery bag.

Jessica chose that moment to walk by on her way to the bathroom. "Fruit?" she said. "You got fruit? Just wait till Rory hears. Boy, she'll be sorry she missed this."

Donnie helped me gather the peaches, plums, and nectarines that rolled under our beds like balls in an arcade machine. And though she clucked with comfort when everyone stared at my tumbling fruit, I feared Donnie regretted she had ever decided to be my friend.

●

I met Erin's parents when the bell rang for morning activity period. Mrs. Hollander, her soft middle hidden by an oversized shirt, hugged me as if I were her child. "It's so nice to meet Erin's best friend," she said. "I don't know what she'd have done without you this summer." I pictured Mrs. Hollander baking cookies, letting Erin eat dough off the mixing spoon.

"Hey, Charlie. This is for you." Erin took a cookie from her pocket and placed it in Charlie's hand as we headed for the campcraft area. Charlie wriggled from my father, who talked with Erin's dad as if they'd known each other for years, and squeezed between Erin and me. Right behind us, Erin's mother told mine how happy she was that Erin and I were friends.

"See, isn't this great? I told you it'd be great," Erin said. "And your mom's really pretty, by the way."

"Thanks." I knew the response, though I didn't know why I had to thank everyone who noticed my mother's looks.

"So didya get everything you wanted?"

"You wouldn't believe what I got," I whispered so my mother wouldn't hear.

Erin pulled out another cookie. "For you."

I couldn't take the offering with Mom looking on. "No thanks. My mother doesn't let me eat sweets." I continued to keep my voice low while I spoke over Charlie's head.

"Sorry, I didn't know. So what'd they bring you?"

"You ready for this? Fruit."

"And what else?"

"Fruit. That's all. Nectarines, peaches, and plums."

"Holy moly! Does Rory know?"

"Not yet. She hasn't been around since cleanup. But she'll hear soon enough." I tightened my hold on Charlie and peeked behind us in case Rory crept up, in case my mother was listening in.

"Not to worry," Erin said. "I've got plenty of stuff for both of us. If anyone asks, just say your parents left your real treats in the car."

●

At campcraft we gathered twigs, then fanned the flame in a stone ring. Mothers stood back and sighed with boredom, while fathers moved in close and grinned as if their daughters had just discovered fire. Charlie, who had sandwiched himself between our father and Erin's, flapped for my attention. "It's okay, buddy," I said when I pulled away from girls mixing pancake batter. "We're getting ready to cook on a campfire. See? And once we make breakfast, you'll get to eat with me. How's that?"

Charlie smiled—a shadow of a smile, really. He looked so sad that I wanted to grab him and run. Run all the way home like Hansel and Gretel.

"Come on, you two," Erin called. "Charlie can help. As we say in my house: The next best thing to a private chef is an extra pair of hands. Right, Mom?"

Erin's mother chuckled as I reworked my daydream. I wouldn't save my brother by running to our house. We would run to Erin's, where Mrs. Hollander would let us eat half the chocolate chips before we mixed any into the cookie dough.

Nancy stopped by before the pancakes were done. She flashed her signature smile at the gathering of parents off to the side of the campcraft area, then squatted beside Charlie. "I'm glad you came to visit," she said, her touch on his back as gentle as her voice. She greeted everyone, reminding fathers they could change into bathing suits in the rec hall bathrooms; mothers would use the nature hut. "And I'll see you all at the lake in a half hour," she said. "Enjoy this lovely day."

It *was* a lovely day, I realized only after Nancy said it was. The sky uncluttered with clouds. The sun just right, warming the air to perfect picnic temperature. Yet I didn't look forward to lunch on the lawn. I wanted to stretch our time at campcraft, away from my mother.

Erin swiped her father's camera and snapped a photo of Charlie and me. Then she helped me explain to him why he had to go with Dad when campcraft ended. I liked how she told Charlie we wanted him to swim with us, and he had to get his suit on before he could go to the lake. "The lake," Charlie whispered. "Swim with Amy." He took my father's hand and headed for the rec hall. No fuss. No scene. If only I could avoid Rory, then maybe visiting day wouldn't be so bad.

Erin walked back to the cabin arm in arm with her mother, chatting as if they were friends. I escorted mine, the silence heavy between us. I thought about the way my mother had barely said "hi" to Donnie and Erin, about the bag of fruit, about Mom and Uncle Ed.

She spoke as we neared senior camp. "It's nice here. Peaceful."

A safe subject. I eked out a simple "Yes."

"You're very quiet."

"Not much to say, I guess," I answered, as the path from campcraft merged with the main path to our cabins. Campers barged in from the athletic areas, arts and crafts, drama, gymnastics. Girls hustled to change for swim, mothers at their sides. I turned at the laughter behind us: Rory and Robin in leotards that cinched their waists and hugged their chests.

"Hi, Aunt Sonia," Robin cried. "Nice skirt." I was certain my mother didn't catch the sarcasm.

I kept walking while she slowed to say hello.

"Don't run off," Rory called. "Introduce me to your mother."

"Looks like you've already met," I said, glancing back as I tried to keep an even gait.

"Don't be rude, Amy," my mother told me. "Wait for Robin and your friend."

"Your pretty mother has pretty good manners," Rory said.

Robin giggled as Rory kept on. "So please introduce us. Then we gotta go. Time to get ready for swim. Your brother's going in the lake with you, isn't he?"

Seniors and their mothers scurried by as Rory, Robin, and my mother closed in on me, trapping me in the woods with no sign of home and only the witch's house ahead. *Nibble, nibble like a mouse. Who is nibbling at my house?* I had to save Charlie. I had to save myself. Shutting my eyes for an instant, I struggled for air. "Mom, this is Rory. Rory, my mother." The words scratched my throat.

"Pleased to meet you," Rory said, as if being a lady came naturally. Then, "You know, Mrs. Becker, something about you reminds me of our counselor, Patsy, who's very pretty too, I might add."

My mother smiled. "Thank you. You're a very sweet girl."

"Well, see you in the cabin, Mrs. Becker. You too, Amy," Rory called as she and Robin ran ahead.

My mother faced me and narrowed her lips. "Now that's the kind of girl to be friends with. She and Robin seem pretty close. I'd like to meet her parents."

"They didn't come."

"What a shame. They're probably fine people."

I was tempted to tell my mother that Rory should win an Academy Award. But instead, I chose silence.

"I don't know what's gotten into you," my mother said as we neared senior camp. "I raised you to have good manners, not to be rude to your friends."

"Rory's not my friend."

"Well, she should be. She's got a lot more on the ball than that Erin."

"You don't know them." My words came clearly, louder than they should have.

"I know enough to say you don't know how to pick the right friends, Amy."

"I know more than you think I do."

"And what does *that* mean?"

Uncle Ed and my mother. Every time I closed my eyes, the memory came back. "Never mind," I answered as we entered Bunk 9.

●

Patsy faced the wall when she changed into her bathing suit. The presence of mothers must have made her modest. Usually Patsy stood bare-chested by her bed a bit longer than necessary, showing off her body—a lesson on what we should aspire to, I figured. This time, though, it was Rory who showed off. She stood facing us, pulling up her suit in slow motion.

Most of the mothers chose not to put suits on. Let the fathers swim with their daughters, they probably decided. Fathers, who wouldn't care how they'd look coming out of the lake. Fathers, who wouldn't have to worry about flattening their hair with bathing caps.

What I worried about as I put on my tank suit was what Rory was planning for Charlie. Clearly, she had played up to my mother for a reason. My mother, who sat at the foot of my bed, her legs crossed as if she were ready to take dictation. I changed facing my robe and laundry bag, avoiding my mother's glance. Rory was gone before I turned around.

"All right, y'all," Patsy called from her side of the cabin. "Let's hurry to the lake. Wouldn't want any o' my gals to be late." Since when did Patsy care whether we were on time?

"You're lucky you have a good counselor," my mother said as she hiked up one of my bathing suit straps to sit higher on my shoulder. Her touch made me tremble. "And she *is* quite attractive. I'm surprised she chose to work at a girls camp."

Erin came in to grab me for swim while Mrs. Hollander waited outside. "My mother says some girls like their privacy, especially at our age," Erin explained.

Mrs. Hollander: not only affectionate but sensitive too. Yes, I imagined, Charlie and I would run away to Erin's house. We'd find out how it would feel to have a real mom.

My mother's voice drew me from this daydream. "You go on with the girls if you want. I'll find my way to the lake."

Charlie and my father met us there. Charlie bounced on the sand as if it were a trampoline. "Hey, buddy. Ready to swim?"

"I could barely keep him from running in." My father looked around at clusters of campers and parents. "Where's Mom?"

I told him she had said I should go on ahead with Erin.

"Well, you know your mother won't be swimming, so maybe I should keep her company while you and Charlie go in. Okay with you, honey?"

"Sure." I answered with the truth for a change. No need for an adult, not even my father. Erin had said she would swim with Charlie and me. Neither of her parents was going in either. We would stay in the crib area. Erin didn't mind.

And Rory and Robin wouldn't swim with the babies. So we'd be safe, at least for now. But I looked around anyway, anxious to see where the enemy hid.

The staff took their positions on the dock. Charlie gave one hand to Erin and one to me. At the sound of the whistle, we ran into the lake. "Cold!" Charlie cried as our feet hit the water. Yet he made no effort to run back.

"Let's find fish," Erin suggested.

"Fish," Charlie repeated, as goose bumps rose on his arms. But the crowd of fathers wading with freshmen campers must have scared off the minnows. "Not to worry," Erin said. "They'll come soon."

Charlie stopped fluttering while I wet his shoulders. I helped him ease into the water. He *had* gotten thinner. No doubt about it. What were meals like for him at home without me, without anyone talking to him at the table? And what if he kept getting thinner—thinner and thinner until he'd nearly disappear? Unless I went home with him. Then he might eat again.

Maybe I was wrong to believe my parents wouldn't let me leave camp. What if I told them about Rory, about the initiation? Would my mother really blame me, or would she allow herself to see my pain? If my parents heard the truth about Takawanda—better yet, if they witnessed it—they might take me home, where I would keep Charlie healthy. I'd be able to endure my mother's criticism, but I might not survive Rory's threats. At home, at least, I'd know what to expect. And at home, I'd help Charlie.

A new plan flooded my mind as I watched Erin splash him. I would catch Rory in a false move all right. Not *her* final move but *my* final one, the last false move I'd see at Takawanda. If Rory tried anything, I decided right then, I'd make sure my parents noticed. I would show them what camp truly was: a war zone in which I was trapped. So what if my parents would learn I had lied? What difference would that make?

"You okay?" Erin patted my shoulder.

"Sure. Why?"

"You got so quiet, like you disappeared or something."

Leave it to Erin. Did she sense she might lose me? I couldn't tell her I had made a new plan, one that didn't need a group or a code word, one in which her only role would be to wish me a good trip home.

Charlie squealed as a school of minnows darted by. "Fish, Amy! Fish!"

I hugged him close. His hair, drenched with spray from the lake, drooped on his forehead. I pushed it back.

"See, I told you not to worry," Erin said. "I knew we'd see fish." She splashed his chest gently—a sprinkle of water, really—as if she knew a big spray might knock Charlie down. He giggled and showered Erin back. "Sometimes, Charlie, my friend," she told him, hiding her eyes from the water he thrust at her with his hands, "you just have to wait for what you want." Erin laughed as Charlie splashed harder, arms in full motion now. "And if you wait long enough, you usually get it."

I thought about how much I would miss Erin when my parents would take me home at the end of visiting day. But I had waited long enough. It was time to get what I wanted.

I waved at Dad, standing near the lake, Uncle Ed beside him. Where was my mother? I scanned the beach, alive with parents.

And where was Rory? For the first time, I wanted her to find me. I wanted her to storm into the lake and shove me. Not Charlie, of course. As much as I yearned to go home, I wouldn't risk Charlie for my cause. But I hoped my father would see Rory attack, see her strike me for no reason. No reason except that thrashing me made her feel good. But where was she?

Erin splashed me hard. "Hey, where are you?"

"Right here." I scooped water and got Charlie's back, then sprayed Erin as if she had it coming, as if she were Rory.

"Well, that's more like it. Let's get her, Charlie!"

A curtain of water came at me. As it lowered, I spotted my mother at the far edge of the beach, shoes in hand, Rory at her side.

Chapter 14

A Liar and a Misfit

That Rory's a nice girl. And pretty too," my mother said as we walked back from the lake. "What a shame her parents couldn't visit."

"She's not, Mom."

"How can you say that, Amy? She's one of the prettiest girls here."

"She's not nice," I said through my teeth. Should I tell the truth now: that I filled my letters with lies about the girls and all the fun we were having?

No time to decide before she spoke again. "Well, Rory's a lot more friendly than the other girls." If I hadn't been so sad, the irony of my mother's focus on friendliness—Rory's friendliness, no less—might have amused me. What did she know about being friendly? My mother, whose shield of ice even Erin hadn't melted. As if my mother had moved into my brain, she continued in a whisper, "Certainly more friendly than that Erin."

I knew what Rory was up to. She had duped my mother to protect herself. Or she had fooled my mother to get to me. "You don't know what Rory's really like," I said.

But my mother didn't give me a chance to tell her. "Maybe if you didn't stick with that Erin all the time, Amy, you would know Rory better—Rory and the other girls. She told me what's been going on. How the only one you're friends with is Erin—no matter what you say in your letters—and I'm not happy about that."

So Rory had blabbed my less-than-popular status. Less than popular with her boy-crazy gang. She had made my mother see me as the misfit, confirming what I knew she already felt. Uncle Ed wouldn't have to tell my parents a thing. A liar and a misfit. That's how he would want me to be seen so his secret would be safe. Who'd believe me now if I snitched on him and Patsy? Patsy, who had already charmed my father. Patsy, who my mother said was a good counselor. Words wouldn't work to get me out of Takawanda. My only hope was for my parents to catch Rory in action.

I shuddered as we approached the cabin. But Rory wasn't there. In Bunk 10 with Robin, I thought. Probably planning a lunch attack, so easy now that my mother was on her side. "You don't have to keep me company while I change," I told her, my hostile tone a surprise even to myself.

"Where else would I go?"

I said nothing as my mother followed me inside. I turned my back, hurried out of my suit, and threw on the camp uniform in record time. While I tucked in my T-shirt, my mother fiddled with the pens and pencils in my cubby, lining them up with all points facing inward.

Mrs. Hollander greeted us outside Bunk 10. "Erin's not dressed yet," she said. "Go on in if you want, hon. I'll wait here with your mother."

For an instant, I forgot about Rory as I raced up the steps to see Erin.

"Well, la-de-da." Rory sat, fully clothed, on Robin's bed. "Yes indeedy. Look what the wind blew in. It's Amy with her tennis racquet. Eager to show off for visitors, huh, Amy Becker? But guess what, fruit girl? No one cares how you play." Aware of Paula's mother in the cabin and moms outside, Rory kept her voice low. "Fruit. Now what kind of parent brings fruit?" Rory and Robin laughed. "I wonder where her pretty mother is?" Rory whispered to my cousin, just loudly enough for me to hear.

"Who cares about Aunt Sonia?" Robin answered in full voice. "Jeez! What an outfit she chose for visiting day. Like she thought she was going to a dance or something. No wonder she sent Amy a dress for the social."

"Stop it, you guys," Erin said as I studied the baking tins on her bed—homemade cookies and brownies, I supposed. I pleaded with Erin to hurry so we could leave. I wasn't looking for trouble in the cabin. I wanted trouble outside, where both of my parents would see it. I had to check the attack until lunch.

"Not so fast," Rory said as soon as Paula and her mother left the cabin. "Let's get something straight. I'm talking to *you*,

Erin. You and the fruit girl. First, we're not your guys. And second, we're not interested in what you have to say. Either of you."

"Let's go!" I held my racquet with one hand, latched on to Erin's arm with the other.

"No. They can't make fun of your mother that way."

"Zip it, Hollander," Rory hissed. "Who's gonna stop us?"

"Come on." I pulled Erin by the wrist.

"At least Amy's mother showed up," Erin shot back. "That's more than I can say for yours."

The sound of a crash followed us out the door. I knew what it was: a baking tin smacked at the wall. Erin's cookies and brownies, broken and smashed, probably dotted the floor.

"What was that?" Mrs. Hollander wanted to know.

"Just Rory," Erin answered. "It stinks, how mean she is."

"But she seems like such a nice girl," my mother said as we walked behind Erin and her mom. "She's probably jealous, that's all." I clenched my fists as my mother kept on. "It must be hard for a camper without parents on visiting day. We should ask her to have lunch with us."

Erin and her mother froze. "Don't you know what's been going on?" Mrs. Hollander turned and asked as campers and mothers, eager for lunch, hurried by at the head of the path. "If I knew that Amy hadn't discussed it with you, then I would have told you."

"I don't know what you're talking about," my mother answered.

Erin's mother locked eyes with me. She knew the truth about Rory. The truth about everything, I imagined, except about Uncle Ed. Erin had agreed not to tell that. Sure, it was okay for me to despise him, but I didn't want the whole world in on his secret. He was family, after all. Dad's family.

"Amy, why haven't you told your mother about Rory?" Mrs. Hollander asked when I looked away.

"I...well...I just haven't had a chance yet." Seniors and mothers wandered ahead. Everyone but Rory and Robin, who stayed behind to steal goodies, no doubt.

"She has to know, hon," Mrs. Hollander said. Her voice sounded as if she were comforting a sick child.

"What about Rory?" my mother asked.

Mrs. Hollander glanced down, offering me a moment to get it out. But I didn't know how to start. How could I explain why I hadn't told my parents about Rory and her gang?

"I've been trying to tell you all morning," I finally said. "Rory's not nice."

Mrs. Hollander hustled Erin ahead, leaving my mother and me behind on the now empty path. We took a few steps in silence, the only sound the crunching of pine needles, laughter up ahead.

"And I've been trying to tell *you*, Amy: Rory says she tried to get to know you, but you didn't make an effort." My mother lowered her voice. "I suppose it's Erin's fault, the way she keeps you to herself. It's obvious she's not a popular girl."

Anger burned in my chest. How could my mother blame Erin for my social standing? I wouldn't let her put down the one person who had jeopardized her own summer by welcoming me on the bus. "You don't know what goes on here." The words spewed out. "And Erin's the nicest person I know."

"But she isn't the kind of person who can help you. You never know when you'll need your friends in order to survive, Amy." Another clue to my mother's history. But trapped in the present, I couldn't think about her past. "And Erin's just not the right girl for you to stick with," my mother went on. "I have no use for her." I thought I heard the period in my mother's voice, but it was only a semicolon. She squared her shoulders and continued, her voice muted, even though Erin and Mrs. Hollander were far in front of us now. "I'm a good judge of character, Amy, and I have no use for her mother either."

That's when I knew I had to prove my mother wrong. We'd been waging our war for years, a war in which she had all the power. Yet she was wrong about Rory, wrong about Erin. Wrong about me. Certainly I was a better judge of character than my mother. I would make her see that, even if it wouldn't get me out of camp. And maybe that was fine. Maybe Takawanda wasn't worse than home, just more open in its battles. If not for Charlie, I might have wanted to stay after all. "You pays your money and you takes your chances." Isn't that what Clarence had said?

●

Uncle Ed smiled when he found my mother and me as we neared the junior camp lawn, where Erin's father spread blankets for our picnic lunch. "Sonia!" my uncle called, his arms outstretched as he rushed toward us. I wished he would stop acting as if he still wanted my mother. Wasn't Patsy enough? "Sorry I couldn't give you a proper greeting at the lake, Sonia. Quite a place I've got here, isn't it?" My mother stiffened in his hug. "And everyone's having a great time." Uncle Ed kept talking as my mother pushed away. "Isn't that so, Amy?" I didn't answer.

In the distance, Charlie and my father stood by the junior camp tetherball. Charlie followed the game with his head as if watching a Ping-Pong match. I told my mother I would get them, but her raised eyebrows stopped me. She didn't want to stay with Uncle Ed any more than I did, and she squirmed around the Hollanders as if Erin's family had an itchy rash. "Excuse me, Ed." The chill in her voice made me shake. "I need to let Lou know we're here."

Erin jumped up as we got close, but Mrs. Hollander held her back. "No, baby. Let's give Amy a little more time with her mother," I thought I heard Mrs. Hollander say as I waved to Erin. Mrs. Hollander probably thought I'd been reporting on what Rory had done. Erin's mom couldn't know that my mother had decided all the problems were Erin's fault for sticking close to me, or my fault for not being popular.

"I just wish you'd choose other friends. Like Rory," my mother said when we wove between blankets and towels spread on the lawn. We skirted the clothed buffet table as we headed for Charlie and my father. "You could do so much better, Amy."

Nothing I could say would convince my mother she was wrong. But she would see for herself soon enough, I believed. Rory would attack during lunch. I was as sure of it as I was that Charlie would race into my arms when he saw us coming.

My father waved as we approached. Charlie sped toward me until the sound of a dog halted his flight. Not a deep bark like Zeus's, the Sparbers' black Lab, but the squealing yap of an itty-bitty thing, as Robin had warned. I ran to my brother and scooped him up. "It's okay, buddy," I crooned as I hugged Charlie, while I scanned younger campers and parents heading for picnic places. I didn't see the dog, though I knew who I'd see where the barking came from. "Hi, Mrs. Becker!" Rory yelled before my father reached us. "All set for lunch?" Robin stood beside her and grinned.

I turned away and hugged Charlie harder. "It's all right now." I whispered my promise: "I won't let them hurt you."

"Why don't we invite Rory to join us for lunch?" my mother suggested when my father caught up with us. "Give Erin's family a little time to themselves."

"That's up to Amy. This is her day." I saw the strain in my father's smile as he looked at me and Charlie. "What do you say, honey?"

"No. I want to sit with the Hollanders." Charlie's arms tightened around me. "Just the Hollanders."

"Okay then." My father patted Charlie's back. "The dog's not here, son, and it's time for lunch now. So let go of Amy."

"No!" Charlie shrieked, not loudly enough to cause a commotion, but forcefully enough so I knew he wouldn't budge. I carried him to the picnic area, now jammed with families. At first no one seemed to notice the eight-year-old who clung to me. Yet for a moment, I wished my father had heeded my letter and left Charlie home. But all thoughts vanished when I heard snickers behind us, clear as the bell that would open the buffet. I knew who it was: Rory and Robin, celebrating the success of the dog scare.

"I still think we should ask Rory to join us," my mother said as we headed toward the Hollanders, "since her parents aren't here."

"Sonia, please, Sonia. Amy wants to be with Erin. What's wrong with that?"

"What's wrong is she doesn't give herself a chance to know anyone else. No wonder she doesn't have friends." My mother spoke as if I weren't even there.

"Of course she has friends. You read her letters." My father turned to me. "And your friends are lucky to have you. Especially Erin. She seems real nice, by the way, and so do her parents."

"They're so ordinary," my mother snapped.

Erin ran over to us. "Hey, Charlie, my friend. Where you been?" She tousled his hair the way I always did, then peeled his arm from my neck and took his hand. Charlie lowered himself and, surrounded by Erin and me, hunkered down at our picnic spot. My father found his place next to Mr. Hollander. My mother positioned herself at the edge of the blanket, her legs tucked to the side like Patsy's at our ice cream party.

I jumped at the sound of the lunch bell.

"Oh my God!" Erin slapped my knee. "Look who's serving!"

Charlie's hands clamped my ankle when I got up to scan the table. Junior counselors and counselors-in-training stood behind platters of fried chicken and baskets filled with rolls. And next to the youngest staff and CITs, Andy and Jed in white aprons.

"Who's hungry?" Erin teased as she released Charlie's hands and pulled him to his feet.

"Stop it. Come on," I said, not wanting my mother to know about Andy.

"What's the secret, girls?" my father asked. "Someone likes those fellows over there?"

"The kitchen boys are *so* nice, Mr. Becker," Erin answered.

"Come on. Stop." I whined my protest, but my father goaded Erin on.

"So which one's the lucky guy? Or are they both?"

I hung my head.

"That good-lookin' one on the right," Erin said, "that's Andy. And he's really nice, and he likes Amy a lot."

"Well, that's great. Shows he's got good taste." My father lifted my chin. "Don't be embarrassed, honey. Why, I'll bet he's a great guy."

My mother shook her head as she rose. "He's a kitchen boy, Lou."

Erin held Charlie's hand when we headed for the lunch line. She steered us toward Andy and Jed's end of the buffet table. Mrs. Hollander followed, while Mr. Hollander and my parents trailed behind. "Andy, that's his name, right? He's awfully cute," Erin's mother whispered.

I took a plate for Charlie and one for myself as we inched along the table. "Hey, Amy." Andy smiled. "I was hoping I'd see you." He surveyed the crowd, scouting for Uncle Ed, I was sure.

Jed stabbed a chicken breast. "How b-b-bout this?"

"Thanks. That's fine for me." I held out Charlie's plate. "And my brother would like a drumstick, if you've got one."

"I d-d-don't th-think we have any more."

"I'll find one," Andy offered. He dashed to the other end of the table before I could say it wasn't necessary.

"Holy moly!" Erin's tap on my shoulder nearly caused me to drop a plate. "He's crazy about you. Isn't he great, Mom?" I peeked around for Mrs. Hollander's answer. And that's when I saw Uncle Ed. He sidled next to my father on the lunch line. "What's the hold up here?" Uncle Ed boomed. Then spotting Andy with a plate of chicken legs, Uncle Ed asked, "What did I tell you about staying at your post and keeping the line moving?"

I felt my uncle's eyes on me as Andy forked two drumsticks onto Charlie's plate. "Let's keep moving," Uncle Ed ordered. "Lots of hungry people here." Andy looked down when I thanked him.

He's a kitchen boy, Amy. I turned, but my mother wasn't behind me. Yet I heard her voice while I balanced Charlie's plate and mine.

"So, Ame," Erin said, as we settled on the blanket ahead of our parents, "didya finally tell your mother about Rory and everything? My mom couldn't believe your mother didn't know what's been happening."

"I tried, but my mother says it's *my* fault."

"*Your* fault? How could it be *your* fault?" Erin twirled a pigtail. "Guess your mother still doesn't know what's really going on then."

Right, I thought. *You don't know anything, Mom. Nothing.*

Chapter 15

What in the World Is Wrong with You?

I looked for Rory as we sang the Takawanda welcome song. But without standing, I saw only the families around us. I searched some more when Nancy instructed us to rise for the alma mater. Charlie stood with me. Was Rory planning to get him again? I had figured she was going to drift by during lunch, but desserts were already out—cake and cookies and watermelon—and still no Rory. And no dog.

"Ready for a little tennis?" my father asked. "My racquet's in the car. I'll go get it."

"Lou." My mother nodded toward Charlie.

"He's fine with the girls."

"Sure he is," Erin agreed. "Aren't you, Charlie? We're gonna watch Amy play tennis."

"Amy. Tennis." Charlie's voice came as a whisper. I didn't think anyone else heard him. But Erin had. "Right," she answered. "Watch Amy play tennis." She pulled Charlie to his feet. "Watch with us," Erin urged her parents.

"Wouldn't miss it," Mrs. Hollander said.

Jody zeroed in on my father and me. She stopped to grab tennis balls from the shopping cart, then ushered us onto the middle court. "It's a pleasure to meet you, Mr. Becker," she said. "Your daughter's a fine player, one of the strongest in camp. And one of the nicest girls too." Jody tossed me the balls. "Now show your father how your time here's paying off."

"Go for it," Erin called. I turned at her voice. She stood in back of Charlie, his nose against the chain link fence behind the courts. Erin's parents stood to her side. No sign of anyone with a dog. No sign of my mother. I bounced a ball—once, twice. Why wouldn't she watch me play?

"Let's see how good you've gotten," Dad teased.

I began hitting slowly, grooving my strokes as he had taught me. Where was Rory?

I heard Erin's mother say I was good. "Wait," Erin told her. "She's just warming up. You haven't seen anything yet."

As if on cue, my father picked up the pace. He slammed a forehand to the baseline. I hit a strong cross-court. "Good shot, honey," he called. "Let's see your backhand."

Erin gave me a thumbs-up when I turned to get a ball. I tickled Charlie's nose, still pressed to the fence. "Love you, buddy," I said, then readied myself to hit by bouncing the ball.

"Stalling for time?" My father chuckled.

"Oh, so you're eager for everyone to see that I'm better than you, Dad?"

Erin laughed at our banter. "Go on, Ame. Show him how good you are."

The racquet became part of me. I fed off my father's pace, returning each shot with a bullet of my own. Applause— louder than Erin's family alone could have given. Campers and parents on the other courts stopped hitting. The strike of the ball. The movement of my feet. That's all there was. *On your toes, Amy. On your toes.* Jody's words in my mind kept me light, made me fly. "One of the strongest players in camp," she had said. "A good bet to win the senior tournament."

I slammed a backhand down the line. "Great shot!" My father clapped the strings of his racquet.

"Way to go!" Erin's voice pulled me back into myself. I glanced behind to catch a smile stretch across her face, Charlie still in front of her, her parents to her left. My mother stood next to them now. She left just enough space between her and the Hollanders so no one would think they were together. And on my mother's other side, Rory and Robin gabbed as if they belonged there. Not an inch between them and my mother.

I took in the crowd fanning out across the fence. No dogs. No barking. Charlie's fine, I assured myself. Erin will protect him.

"Stalling for time again?" my father kidded.

Rory won't hurt Charlie now, I decided, shaking off my fear of another attack. He looked so peaceful up against the fence, Erin's hands gentle on his shoulders. *Show Mom how good you've gotten*, I told myself. *Show her you're special. Hit the ball, Amy. Smack it hard.*

I whammed a forehand down the center, a backhand to the corner. Yet despite my shots, the audience thinned. Campers pulled their parents away until not one spectator remained to Erin and Charlie's right.

I waited a moment to see if my mother would stay. Though she didn't move from her position near the Hollanders, I knew she had no interest in watching me. My mother wouldn't care that I was one of the best players in camp. What good was tennis if I wasn't friendly enough or pretty enough or popular enough? Yet I wanted her to hear the "Great shot!" and "What a player!" I wanted her to know that some people thought I was good enough at something.

"What's the matter? Tired already?" My father seemed to enjoy the spotlight we shared. He was proud of my playing. He had taught me well. Not bad for a father who never had time for his own game. Not bad for a man upstaged his whole life by his kid brother, Eddie Becker, the boy the girls came to watch, as my father had said. Uncle Ed, whose own daughter, with private tennis lessons and indoor winter practice, had to fight to keep up with me on the court.

I started a rally, but my focus scattered. The Hollanders still applauded, and my mother stood, straight as a pine tree, in her spot. But Rory and Robin were gone.

I should have left the court when I saw they weren't there. Yet Charlie seemed fine. And I wanted my mother to see that tennis wasn't a waste—not for me, anyhow. *Focus. Concentrate. Make Mom see you're special.*

I tried again to shrink my universe to the ball spinning toward me. *Racquet back. Step. Swing.* A shot to my father's backhand. I tracked the ball, heard the thump of his contact. Then Charlie screamed.

I spun around as a tan dog zoomed in from the right, claiming Charlie before Erin saw it coming. The cocker spaniel jumped and barked. It licked Charlie's leg. I dropped my racquet and ran from the court. "Get him off!" I yelled to Erin. She grabbed the dog's collar while my mother squeezed in front of Mr. and Mrs. Hollander. By the time I circled behind the fence, my mother held Charlie from the back, her arms binding his chest as if trying to hold his wails in. Long, howling cries—a huge sound from such a little boy. Louder than the barking, which hadn't stopped, though Erin held the dog at a distance now.

I didn't pay attention to the gathering of campers and parents as I lifted my brother. "It's all right, buddy. I've got you." My words did nothing to thaw his frozen body, nothing to stop his shrieks. "See, buddy, no more dog. You're okay now."

My father, who had raced on my heels, tried to help. "Calm down now, son. See?" He pointed to Erin. "The dog's way over there. Erin's holding him so he can't get near you."

"Sorry. I'm really, really sorry," Erin called. "I got him off as fast as I could."

"It's not your fault," I told her, knowing who was responsible. Surely Rory had masterminded the attack.

Something else I knew too: Charlie's screams could go on for an hour. And with each new yell, with every "No!"—as if my brother still felt the dog on his leg—my anger doubled.

Let Rory threaten me all she pleased, whip me all she wanted. But Charlie? She couldn't hurt him and get away with it. I wouldn't allow that.

"Does anyone know whose dog that is?" Uncle Ed marched across the field, Nancy beside him. "Who owns that dog?" He veered toward the rec hall, leaving Nancy to disperse campers and parents, still huddled around us. "Mr. and Mrs. Becker," she said, "I'm so sorry about this." I tried not to meet Nancy's eyes, couldn't risk crying. "I'm going to find out who that dog belongs to," she went on, patting Charlie's shoulder. I knew he didn't feel her touch.

"Why don't you find Rory and ask *her* whose dog it is?" Though I wasn't angry with Nancy, I finally unmuzzled my rage.

"Amy!" my mother said.

"What? Rory did this, and she's gonna pay."

Charlie started to shake.

"Now look what you've done." My mother reminded me this was my fault as much as Rory's. If I hadn't been showing off on the tennis court, maybe Rory wouldn't have struck.

"Sonia, please, Sonia." Then, as if Dad read my mind, he said, "None of this is Amy's fault."

Maybe he was right. Maybe Rory would have found a way to get Charlie no matter where I had been and what I had done. I turned to Nancy. "Rory and Robin can tell you whose dog they borrowed for this stunt, and where—"

"Amy!" My mother cut me off. "What in the world is wrong with you? What could Rory and your cousin have to do with that dog?"

I couldn't stop myself. "What's wrong with *you*, Mom? You think that dog just came out of nowhere?"

"Don't use that tone on your mother, young lady." My father made it clear I had gone too far.

"Amy, this isn't getting us anywhere." Nancy sounded annoyed, like when I hadn't told her about Rory emptying my trunk. But now things were different. This time I wanted to tell—no, *needed* to tell—and no one would listen. "I think we're upsetting your brother even more," Nancy said. "So I'm going to go take care of this. I'll be back."

"Find Rory," I called after her, issuing the order as if I were the one with a clipboard. "Ask *her* whose dog she borrowed."

Charlie trembled in my arms as I spoke, though his crying weakened. "Get down now, son," my father told him.

"No."

"Come on, Charlie." My father tried to coax him from me. "That dog can't get you anymore."

"No. No!" Charlie's arms tightened around me as Uncle Ed approached. No wink, just a subtle shake of his head. And not a word to my mother as my uncle pulled my father behind the far court. I didn't care anymore what he might say about me. All I wanted was for my mother to know the truth. All I wanted was for Rory to be punished.

I thought I heard laughter. I looked in the direction of the dog, Erin and her parents restraining it, the spaniel nothing but a playful pup. And skipping toward it, Rory, Robin, and Susie Barr, one of Robin's bunkmates. "Well, there you are, Tiger," Susie sang out. "We thought we'd lost you."

"Oh, hi, Mrs. Becker," Rory shouted as if surprised to see us. "Hope Susie's dog wasn't a problem. Her parents are visiting in her sister's bunk, so we took Tiger for a walk. He loves little kids. And somehow he just got loose. We've been looking all over for him." Rory broke away from her friends and stepped closer to us.

I worked Charlie's arms from my neck and lowered him to his feet. He didn't resist, didn't cry out or shake. He just stood like a twig.

"You're a stupid liar, Rory!" I screamed, hoping everyone would hear me. "Stay away from my family! Stay away from me!" I needed to hit something, but there was nothing to punch. I picked up a pinecone and threw it at Rory's chest.

"Amy!" my mother shouted as Rory laughed.

I pounded my thighs while Rory sauntered behind us toward Jessica and her parents, at the side of the tennis courts. "*She* did this to Charlie," I said. "She told me she would get him. That's why I sent that letter." My words flowed, unstoppable now. "That's why I didn't want Charlie to visit."

I couldn't guess what made him run then. Was it my anger? What I said? I didn't know exactly what Charlie understood that day. He raced off as if he suddenly realized I couldn't protect him anymore, breaking the thread that had tied us together. He zoomed away before my mother or I could grab him. He ran smack into Uncle Ed.

I wasn't the only one who watched my uncle lift Charlie and hold him out as if he were a stranger's baby with a dirty diaper. Rory stopped before she reached Jessica's family. She studied Charlie as his fists punched the air and his legs kicked hard. With Charlie's back to me, I didn't see my brother's face, but I knew what Rory saw. I had seen it in a photo my father had shown me, a picture he kept in his night table drawer: an old photo of himself and his little brother Eddie. When my father showed it to me, I felt him slide into the past—to that stoop in Brooklyn, where he'd sat with a hand on his kid brother's shoulder. "Lucky Charlie," my father had said to me as he shook off the memory. "He's got those handsome Becker genes like your Uncle Ed."

"Put him down," my mother called now to my uncle. I stepped in Charlie's direction, but my mother forced me back. "Your father will handle this."

Dad took Charlie and hugged him close, Charlie limp in his arms. Only then did my mother and I move toward them. I placed my hand on my brother's back and tried to rub trust into him again. "I'm so sorry, buddy," I whispered.

Uncle Ed didn't hug my mother when he told her it was time for my parents to take Charlie home. I watched my uncle approach the Hollanders. They hustled Erin away on what must have been Uncle Ed's command. No sign of the dog or Robin. No sighting of Rory.

"Please get my racquet, Ame." My father sounded as if he could sleep for a week. "And then walk us to the car."

"Ed has no right to make us go early," my mother said. "What will everyone think if we don't stay for the afternoon?" It didn't surprise me that she seemed more concerned about what others would think than she was about Charlie or me. Couldn't she see he was wiped out by fear? And didn't she care about leaving me without visitors for the afternoon?

"This is Ed's camp," my father reminded her. "And it doesn't matter what everyone thinks."

Charlie's vacant gaze told me his visit had already ended. I let myself cry when I picked up my father's tennis racquet. I hadn't pushed the witch into the oven. I hadn't saved my brother.

We walked slowly to the car, Charlie between my father and me. Charlie's hand felt like rubber in mine. His head bowed in defeat. My mother stepped behind us. She carried the canvas bag she'd been toting around, packed with bathing suits and towels.

"Let me go home with you. Please, Dad." The words tumbled out. "I hate camp. I don't want to stay here."

"I know you've had a hard time, honey. Uncle Ed told me you've had problems adjusting. But I don't understand why you said you were having fun."

How could I tell him that I had needed my mother to think I was popular, and that I hadn't wanted to upset him with the truth? "I don't know," I answered, sniffling back tears. "But I'm telling the truth now, Dad. I hate this place! I hate Rory! I just want to go home."

"Did you ask to go home?" My mother hadn't missed a word.

"Please, Sonia. Let me take care of this. You don't know what Ed told me."

"I don't care what Ed told you. Amy has to learn to make friends. She can't just come home." My mother moved next to Dad and talked to him as if I had already gone back to the cabin. "She has to learn to be friends with the right people, people who can help her get ahead in this world."

"Please, Dad," I tried again in my smallest voice. "Please take me home."

My mother wouldn't quit. "I told you before, Amy, you have to get along with all kinds of people to survive. And Rory doesn't seem nearly as bad as you make her out to be."

"Just try to enjoy the second half of the summer," my father said, telling me my mother had already given her ruling. "I understand why you want to come home, Ame, but your mother knows what she's talking about. You have to learn to deal with the Rorys in this world. If your mother hadn't known that, she might not be here today.

"And anyhow, honey, you're playing great tennis. You really could win the tournament. And wouldn't that be something?

"So please tell Erin's family we're sorry we didn't get to say good-bye. They're nice people, the Hollanders. But your mother's right: You need to make other friends too. And truthful letters from now on. Okay?"

If I tried to answer, I wouldn't have been able to stop my tears. So I simply hugged my father when we got to the car. "I love you, Ame," he said. "I wish we could stay." He reached for Charlie.

"Wait," I cried, bundling my brother in my arms. But Charlie didn't blend into me, not even when I said, "I love you, buddy. I'm so sorry."

"Make an effort, Amy," my mother ordered. "Maybe Robin can help you get to know her friends better. Share the fruit with them."

"Nobody wants fruit." The truth kept pouring out as my father got Charlie settled in the car. "And Robin won't help me. Who do you think told Rory about Charlie and dogs?"

"What happened could have been an accident, like Rory said. You don't know anything for sure, Amy."

"I know more than you think, Mom."

"What are you talking about?"

I lowered my voice. "I know about you and Uncle Ed."

My mother got into the car without even waiting for my father to open the door for her. And when my father hugged me good-bye, I knew *he* hadn't heard a word.

Chapter 16

Enough!

"Interesting visiting day," Rory said at dinner. "Wasn't it, Patsy?"

"I know I told you to stay clear of Amy and her family," Patsy answered.

"But who could resist Amy's mother in that party skirt? And cute little Charlie-boy? Come on, Patsy. How could you expect me to stay away from him?"

Rory's words crushed me. I stayed silent at the table.

"Karen, please pass the sandwiches," Patsy said, refusing Rory's bait for her own protection, and, maybe, for mine. Yet I didn't need Patsy to play counselor anymore. I no longer feared Rory. I just hated her.

"See," Donnie said, "what they do with the menu on visiting day? Chicken dinner at lunch, so parents think we're eating great. And after they leave, disgusting sandwiches for supper."

"But dinner doesn't matter, does it?" Rory grabbed her opportunity. "'Cause if we don't eat, I'm sure Amy will share her yummy fruit with us. Am I right or am I right?"

Rory didn't know I had already thrown the fruit into the outdoor trash bin. I only wished my mother could have seen me toss her precious peaches, plums, and nectarines in with candy wrappers and empty cookie bags. At the bottom of my fruit bag, I found two chocolate Tootsie Pops. When had my father sneaked those in?

"You watch your tongue, Rory," Patsy ordered now at our table, "or Mr. Becker'll hear about this."

"But it's not *my* tongue Mr. Becker cares about, is it?" Though Rory's war with me had ended when she got Charlie, she kept up her battle with Patsy. Nothing to lose, Rory probably figured. Uncle Ed wouldn't kick her out now that she was Robin's best friend.

"Enough!" Patsy banged her fist on the table. Silverware jumped, but none of us did. Immune to this sparring, we just slathered mustard on sandwiches and reached for potato chips.

"But I'm not done," Rory said, eager to rouse us. Though I pretended not to listen, her words chilled me. "See," she went on, "I keep picturing Charlie-boy, and I figured out who he reminds me of: Mr. Becker—and I don't mean Amy's father. Yes indeed, little Charlie-boy could be Robin's brother, all right. Catch my drift, Patsy?"

"Stop it right now, Rory! That's Amy's family you're talkin' 'bout again."

I felt Rory's eyes on me. "Doesn't seem to bother Amy."

"Nope. I don't care." My voice came small but free of tears. I picked up my sandwich and chewed on my father's words: "handsome Becker genes like your Uncle Ed." And Rory's observation: "little Charlie-boy could be Robin's brother." I had caught Rory's drift all right, and the question it carried lodged in my gut. I tried to drown it with bug juice, but it stuck with me, trapped for the next four weeks. "Let her say what she wants," I told Patsy.

My battlefield had changed. The opening strike: telling my mother I knew about her and Uncle Ed. Revenge for her not having seen the truth about camp. My mother didn't believe that Rory staged the dog attack. She couldn't understand my wanting to come home. And when I told her I knew her secret, my mother said nothing.

What would happen at the end of the summer? How much longer could my mother and I keep dancing around each other before we'd finally crash?

●

Rory chose a new target after visiting day—a double: Fran and Karen. I got tired of Rory's telling them to shut their traps. And when she intercepted Fran's mail and ordered Jessica to tear it up, I spoke out. "Don't listen to her, Jess," I called from my bed.

"Well, la-de-da," Rory jumped in. "Look who's looking for trouble."

"No trouble," I answered, my voice strong and even. "I just don't see what's in it for you."

"That's none of your business now, is it, Amy Becker?"

"Nope. I suppose not. But I just thought you'd come up with something new instead of stealing mail again, Rory."

"You know, Jess, she's got a point. I'll come up with some-thing new all right. Maybe try it out on Amy."

"What do I care?" I answered, looking down at the letter from my father. "Do whatever you want."

Dear Amy,

    I'm sorry you're still not having fun. I was hoping things would get better after visiting day. But at least you've got the tennis matches to look forward to. You're playing great, and if you hit like you did with me, I bet you'll win the tournament.

    Mom said to tell you she hopes you enjoy the last two weeks of camp. She still thinks you'd be happier if you made new friends. So please try, honey. I'm sure there are plenty of nice girls there. By the way, Mom's surprised you haven't written anything about the fruit we brought. She wants to know if all the girls enjoyed it.

    Charlie's fine now, so don't worry about him. I'm sure he's forgotten all about that dog. He's even sleeping better. I guess he's finally used to your being away. But I know he'll be happy when you get home. So stop worrying and just have fun. That's what you're there for.

    Good luck in the tournament! My money's on you, Ame.

Love and kisses,
Dad

●

Erin and I continued to meet in the boathouse. I didn't worry that Uncle Ed might find us. Like Rory, he no longer had power over me. Let him tell my father I still don't fit in. Let him tell my mother I'm not popular. So what? Even if my uncle had barged into the boathouse with Patsy, I wouldn't have winced.

All I wanted was to win the tennis tournament and get back to Charlie. At lights out, I would X over the date on my countdown on the last page of my writing pad. As I moved the pen back and forth until black lines nearly tore the paper, I hoped that my brother had really forgotten the cocker spaniel and that he would trust me again. I decided I would give him the tennis trophy if I won it, sort of a reverse homecoming gift.

Cousin Robin and I made it to the finals. Everyone from Bunks 9 and 10 crammed behind the fence, gathering as they had at The Lodge before the Saginaw boys arrived, an invisible line dividing our tribes.

My heart raced when Jody opened a new can of balls, signaling the importance of this match. "Take a five-minute warm-up," she told us. "Good luck."

"I don't need a warm-up," Robin called, playing to her group before she even hit a ball.

"Yes indeedy, Amy Becker," Rory yelled. "Robin's ready for you. No warm-up."

"Amy," Jody said matter-of-factly, "start the warm-up, please. Five minutes."

"Come on, Amy!" Erin cheered as soon as play began. "Hit like you did on visiting day." Visiting day, when I drilled the ball at my father and knew he was proud. Visiting day, when I knew my mother didn't care to watch. My mother, who hadn't even denied her relationship with Uncle Ed.

"Kill her, Robin!" Rory cried.

Focus. Concentrate. Don't let her win.

"Ready?" Robin shouted across the net on her first service game when she led one game to love. "'Cause you're about to see things your father never taught you."

Hit the ball, Amy. Smack it hard. I made a good return. Erin cheered me on with a "Great hit!"

"Great hit!" a male voice echoed. Oh my God. Andy had come to watch. "Clarence gave me the afternoon off," I heard him tell Jody. "I won't be in the way."

Robin refused to shake my hand when I beat her, eight games to three. She stormed away with Rory and their group before I even left the court. Good thing, because Andy and my friends were waiting to congratulate me. Now I could enjoy the attention without hassle.

"Great playing," Andy said. He kissed my cheek, even though I was a sweaty mess. "I'm sorry the summer's almost over," he whispered, then raced away before I could think of what to say.

"I knew you'd win," Erin said. She hooked her arm around my waist as our group headed off to change for swim. "And you lucky duck, your boyfriend was there to see it."

We burst into singing "The Lion Sleeps Tonight," our new favorite song.

Nothing would ruin this day for me. At least that's what I thought.

Chapter 17

You Don't Know Anything

Robin met me at the clothesline. "So tell me the truth," she said. "Your father didn't really teach you, right? You've been taking tennis lessons."

"No, I told you. I learned to play from my father."

"Yeah, like I really believe Uncle Lou could teach you enough to beat me."

"Well, he did." I grabbed my bathing suit and turned toward the cabin.

"Not so fast, cuz." Robin stepped in front of me as if guarding me in basketball. She swiped the suit from my hand. "I'm talking to you. And when I'm finished, you'll get your faggy suit back."

"But we have nothing to talk about. I won fair and square."

"You call that fair and square when you don't tell the truth? If I knew you took lessons, I would've played harder. I could have won, you know."

"But you didn't." I kept my voice strong as girls started to gather for this final battle of the summer.

"Not so loud. We don't need a crowd to work this out."

"Work what out? I'm just a better player than you are." I barely recognized this fearless Amy who spoke up now.

Robin crumpled my bathing suit. "I said I want the truth. So, really, how long have you been taking lessons?"

"Robin, for the last time, my father taught me. Why can't you understand that?"

"'Cause your father's a loser."

Let my cousin say anything she wanted now about my mother. But about Dad? "Well, obviously my father's a better teacher than your private one," I said, "because the match is over, and look who the loser is."

"How dare you talk to me like that!" Robin yelled, no longer caring about keeping voices down. "And how dare you embarrass me on the court in front of my friends. You're the one who should be embarrassed. You and your stupid mother and your loony brother."

"Whaddaya doin' out there, gals?" Patsy called from the cabin.

"How 'bout minding your own business," Rory answered. She stood next to Robin now. "We don't need a counselor watching us our last couple of days."

"*You* need a counselor watching you all the time," Patsy fired back. Laughter and applause from my group, clustered around me. "Get your suits and change for swim," Patsy ordered.

"Go away," Robin told her crowd, including Rory.

"Go ahead," I told my friends. I wasn't looking to make this bigger than it was. Camp was almost over. The tournament was finished. The only thing left was getting home to Charlie.

Erin looked at me. "Robin's just mad I beat her," I explained. "I'll see you in a few minutes."

"Like I said," Robin went on when everyone left, "I could have won. I should have won."

"Why are you making a big deal out of this?"

"Because I still don't believe you didn't take lessons. I know your crazy family, always hiding what you don't want people to find out. Your mother. Now you. You're just like her, you know. Little Miss Perfect. Goody-two-shoes Amy and perfect Aunt Sonia. What a pair. You make me sick, both of you. All your little secrets. All the things we're not allowed to talk about."

"Robin, I swear I don't know what you mean."

"Yeah, right. You are such a liar. You know what secrets I'm talking about."

What secrets? I had to find out. Was this the conversation Robin had tried to start the first time we played tennis? I couldn't have pushed her then, at the beginning of the summer, to tell me what she meant. I couldn't have admitted she knew something I didn't, something about my mother. But everything had changed now that camp was ending. It no longer mattered if I fed Robin's power. My cousin wasn't the enemy. Even Rory wasn't the enemy anymore. My real enemy was my mother. And my memory of her and Uncle Ed made me the powerful one. If there were more secrets, I wanted to know them. The more secrets I gathered, the more powerful I'd be. The more ammunition I would have when I'd need it.

My mother spoke in my head. *You don't know anything, Amy. Nothing.*

"What secrets?" I finally asked Robin.

"You know damn well. Who cares if your mother was married before. And that other daughter? Why the hell does everyone have to be nice to poor Aunt Sonia because of that? 'Think of what she's been through,' my father says. 'Show some compassion, Robin.' As if my father thinks I'm too dumb to see what's going on. As if I don't notice how he practically drools whenever your mother's around." Robin pitched my bathing suit at me. It fell at my feet, which stuck to the ground. "If my father thinks your mother's so great," Robin kept on, her voice softer now, "then let him have her. That's what I say. It doesn't matter to me what they do. And about that baby? Just give me one good reason why I should care. 'Cause I don't feel one bit sorry for your mother. She didn't have to leave that baby in Germany, you know. From what I hear, they all could have gotten out together. Even *my* stupid mother wouldn't leave her baby behind."

My knees buckled when I picked up my bathing suit. What was Robin talking about? I closed my eyes for a moment, then forced myself into the cabin.

"Why, whatever happened to you?" Patsy asked. "You look like you've seen a ghost."

"Tired from my match." I choked on the words, each one a stone in my throat.

"Your cousin must feel mighty sorry for you to let you beat her like that," Rory taunted, handing me a challenge I refused as I sank to my bed. My mother married to someone else? Another daughter? It was too much for Robin to make up. I tried to change for swim, but the cabin whirled around me.

"Are you all right?" Erin asked when she bounced in to meet me. "You don't look good. Can I get you an aspirin or something?"

There was nothing Erin could get me. Nothing anyone could do. The one thing I needed, the truth about my mother, I would get for myself.

I told Erin I'd catch up with her at the lake. "And don't worry. I'm fine."

My final lie of the summer, the biggest yet. How could I be fine when my mother had a life I didn't know about? When I had a sister I'd never even heard of? My mother's secret with Uncle Ed was shameful enough. What else had she hidden from me?

•

At our last breakfast, Patsy told us she'd be right pleased to give us her address "in case any o' you gals have a mind to write me." We waited for Rory to say it wasn't *us* Patsy would want to hear from, was it now? But Rory just kept her head down and twirled the spoon in her cereal bowl.

Andy showed up as we boarded the buses. No kiss this time. Too many onlookers, I guessed. He handed me a small notepad and a stubby pencil. "Can I have your address?" he asked, his voice low. I wrote fast, eager to get it down before Uncle Ed might spot us.

"Come on, campers. Everyone on the buses," Pee-Wee called while I was writing. "No lollygagging now. See you next summer."

"I hope I see you again," Andy said when I gave him the notepad. Without even thinking, I stood on tiptoes and kissed him smack on the lips.

The bus ride home felt shorter than the ride to camp. Erin and I sat up front. "Andy's great, Ame," she said. "I really hope you see him again someday."

Chanting came from behind us. "Amy and Andy sitting in a tree, k-i-s-s-i-n-g."

I didn't mind at all. In fact, I smiled. Andy really liked me, and camp was finally over. And I had kissed him. Wow!

Nancy sat across the aisle from Erin and me. She was keeper of the cookies on this trip. And this time, no one would stop our indulgence. "I worried about you two," Nancy confided, "but look how things worked out. You got to be great friends, you learned to take care of yourselves, and Amy won the tennis trophy. Not bad, I'd say."

After the first rest stop, Nancy gave out lunches. We ate and we sang, though I joined in only when I felt like it or when Erin elbowed me. I no longer needed a chorus of friends.

"I'll miss you two," Nancy said once we hit the city. "And I don't know if I'll be able to give you a proper good-bye when you get off; I'll be making sure everyone's accounted for. So I just want to thank you for all those rest hour visits." She reached over and touched my shoulder.

"Thanks for being there, Nancy," I said. "I don't know what I'd have done without you. And without Erin. I wouldn't have made it through."

"Sure you would've," Nancy answered. "You're a lot stronger than you think. But you can't be afraid to ask for what you need. Remember what I said about the volcano? Call for help before the lava flows."

Sound advice. If only I had listened.

Chapter 18

I Opened the Lid

Erin hugged me before she raced to her mother. I called to Charlie, wrapped around my father's leg. I expected my brother to zoom over, but he stayed where he was. When I melted into my father's arms, Charlie pushed between us. "Hey, buddy." I rumpled his hair. "I couldn't wait to see you. I've missed you so much. And I've got something for you in my bag." I pointed to the carry-on I had dropped at Dad's feet. "Wanna see?"

"He hasn't been himself," my mother explained when Charlie didn't answer.

I stood and faced her. "What do you mean?"

"How about giving your mother a proper hello first?" Did my father believe my mother and I had forgotten to greet each other? Couldn't he see we had chosen not to?

I pecked her cheek. "Welcome home," she said.

I squatted down by Charlie. "So what's going on, buddy? Aren't you happy to see me?" Still no reply, though he let me take his hand.

"Amy should say good-bye to her friends before we go," my mother said when Dad picked up my bag. Not a suggestion but a command. I ignored it as I took in the scene around me: families hugging and talking and laughing; Rory standing alone, no one to welcome her; Nancy weaving through the crowd, checking off names of campers as parents claimed them. She waved as she came toward us. "Mr. and Mrs. Becker. And Charlie. I'll bet you're glad Amy's home." Nancy put a mark on her clipboard—by my name, no doubt. I flashed back to my mother ticking off items when I'd packed them in my trunk. Four pairs of shorts. Check. Ten pairs of underpants. Check. How could that have been only a couple of months ago? Now Nancy marked my name. Amy Becker. Check.

She shifted her clipboard and shook my father's hand. "So nice to see you again," Nancy said. "And you should be very proud of your girl here. Did she show you her trophy?" Without pause, Nancy smiled at my mother. "You've raised a terrific daughter, Mrs. Becker. I'm really going to miss her." I would miss Nancy, I realized—her affection, her concern.

"Hey, Charlie!" Erin called.

Mrs. Hollander greeted my parents. She held me close for a moment, then told Erin to say good-bye. "Friends forever," Erin said as we hugged and cried.

It wasn't saying good-bye to Erin, though, that made my tears come. It was seeing Charlie.

"What's going on, buddy?" I asked again once we settled in the car.

"The summer school teacher says he's been in his own world since we got back from Maine," my mother answered for him. "More so than usual." She pushed her voice over city traffic as she focused out the front window. My mother didn't seem to mind that Charlie could hear us talking about him.

I leaned forward and spoke softly in case he was listening. "What else did the teacher say?"

"I don't know, Amy. What difference does it make?" Not even home yet, and my mother was annoyed. "There are only three more days of summer program. Then he's off for a week before you both go back to school." *He*, as if my brother had no name. I hated that my mother spoke as if Charlie weren't present, as if he didn't understand. Now more than ever, I hated my mother.

How could she have a whole other family I didn't know about? Had my mother told Uncle Ed while they were having their little affair? And had he told Robin? Surely my father knew what had happened to my mother in Germany. "Your mother doesn't talk about that" was his only answer the few times I'd asked about her past.

"Did something happen in summer school, buddy?" I reached across the car and patted Charlie's legs, though they barely jiggled. What I needed to find out was if Charlie still pictured the dog. The dog that was my fault, really. Because that dog wouldn't have had a chance if I wouldn't have been on the tennis court. I didn't want to believe Charlie held on to that fear. And I didn't want to think my yelling at Rory had frightened him so much he withdrew from me still. "Anything happen in school, buddy?" I asked again.

My mother turned in her seat. "You know that's not it. It was visiting day."

"Sonia, please, Sonia. Can't you forget it and just enjoy having Amy back?"

Of course my mother couldn't forget it. And she couldn't forget I knew about her and Uncle Ed. But now I knew other secrets too. Now I chased the ghosts of my mother's past. Yet before I could catch them, I would win Charlie back.

He sat so still, nose pressed to the car window, while Dad and I talked about the tennis matches. My mother stayed as quiet as Charlie when I described the last one. "The trophy's right here in my bag," I told my father.

"We'll see it at home," my mother said. "Your father has to concentrate on driving."

"But I want to show it to Charlie. He can keep it in his room."

"We'll see it later."

Slapped by the period in my mother's speech, we drove the rest of the way in silence. But I heard a voice, as clear as if Rory had pushed into our car. *Cat got your tongue, Amy Becker?*

Rory and I had played our own version of hide-and-seek, I saw then. Like my mother, Rory stole my voice, then forced me to find it. *Well, la-de-da. Am I right or am I right?* One, two, three. *Yes indeedy. Little Charlie-boy could be Robin's brother.* Four, five, six. *Catch my drift, Amy Becker?* Seven, eight, nine, ten. Almost home. Ready or not, here I come.

●

"Welcome home," my father cried when we pulled into the driveway. "I'll bring your bag up for you."

"Amy can manage herself," my mother said. "She might want a little privacy."

Since when was she concerned about my privacy? Hers, yes. Her secrets, her whole other life. But mine? It's not my privacy she's worried about, I thought. It's what I might say to my father if she leaves us alone.

But I had decided not to tell Dad about my mother and Uncle Ed. Why hurt my father when the enemy was my mother? Yet I should have told him about those secrets Robin had shared. The lava was already flowing. I should have asked for help.

"You get organized, and I'll be up soon," Dad called as I climbed the stairs, Charlie behind me.

"I'll see you in a minute, buddy," I said when I opened my door. Something cold and hard settled in my chest as I took in my room. I fingered the Russian dolls on my dresser, stopping at the next-to-the-smallest one. It cracked open with barely a touch, revealing that tiniest doll I had left trapped inside. I cradled the baby in my palm, amazed at the ease with which it had tumbled out, then lined it up with the others. I kicked off my shoes and plunged to my bed, where I snuggled with Puppy. "I'm home," I whispered to my oldest stuffed animal. Home, where I would learn the truth about my mother. Home, where I would get Charlie to trust me again. We had time before the beginning of school. A whole week to build with his blocks, to kick a ball around the backyard, to go for ice cream at night—if my father would take us; if my mother would let him. Two items on my imaginary clipboard: find my mother's past and right my brother's present. I would check them off, I believed, starting now.

I padded into Charlie's room in my stocking feet. He sat cross-legged on the floor, a rectangular block in his hand. "Look what I have." I held out the trophy as an offering. He glanced at me, then lowered his head. "I won this for you, buddy. Want it on your shelf?"

No show of excitement. Not a flapping of arms. I curled next to Charlie and placed the trophy in front of him. "Look, buddy. I won it playing tennis. So why don't we build a fort and put the trophy inside? We've still got a while till Mom calls us for supper."

Charlie fingered my gift: a golden girl, racquet skyward, ready to serve. She stands on a wooden base, a plaque glued to its front. *Camp Takawanda for Girls. Senior Champion. 1963.* "It's for you," I said again. I placed my hand gently on his head and waited a moment before tousling his hair. "A tennis trophy."

Charlie picked it up as if it were a jewel. "Amy. Tennis," he whispered.

I choked back tears. "That's right. I played tennis at camp. And now I'm home." I pulled my brother close in a promise I would be there for him always.

●

The next morning, Charlie hugged me when the minibus came. "Only three more days of summer school, buddy. Then we'll have a whole week together."

With Charlie off to school and my father at the office, my mother and I worked at avoiding each other. I hid in my room, where memories played in my mind: the initiation; Rory at the ice cream party; Andy at the social, on visiting day, at my tennis match; Uncle Ed and Patsy.

I listened for footsteps before I came downstairs to make myself something for lunch. *Let Mom be doing laundry,* I prayed. *Let her be in the basement.* We had barely spoken since I'd gotten home. Better not to say anything, I decided, until I knew as much as Robin.

On the camp bus, I had figured out how to get what I needed. If my mother had a secret family, there'd be proof: photos, letters, birth certificates maybe. And if those clues existed, I knew just where I would find them.

Alone at the kitchen table, I thought again about what my cousin had said. A husband in Germany. Another daughter. How was that possible?

My mother carried up the laundry basket as I finished my sandwich. "Find everything you need?" she asked.

Not yet, but I will, I vowed to myself as I grunted a "Yeah."

Later that afternoon, my mother announced she was going marketing. "Take your time," I told her. "I'll look out for Charlie."

"The summer driver's not as good as the regular one," my mother reminded me. "Sometimes he pulls away before I get to the curb."

"Don't worry." I tried to smooth the edge in my voice. "I'll be out there."

From my bedroom window, I watched the Impala roll down the driveway, then forced myself to wait. I had to make sure my mother wouldn't come back in for a coupon she might have forgotten or to count the eggs in the refrigerator. Sitting on my bed, I listened to the hum of the house and thought about what Erin might be doing. Probably shopping with her mother, buying school clothes, I assumed. They would stop at a coffee shop on their way home, order pie à la mode, and laugh about something Erin said or a silly TV show her mother had seen. Erin would go on about the last half of camp while eating all the ice cream off her pie. Then Mrs. Hollander would spoon over some of hers.

•

I checked my clock, the same one that had awakened me the morning I left for camp. My mother had been gone more than five minutes. It was safe now. Time to find out who she was.

I crept downstairs to my parents' room. My mother's closet door groaned when I opened it. I pulled the chain to turn on the light. It shone on a lineup of shoes: brown high heels and navy pumps; black patent leather and tan sandals; the white flats my mother had worn on visiting day. Each perfectly positioned, toes and heels aligned. A sentry of shoes guarding her metal box. I moved them aside, careful to memorize where each pair belonged—slippers next to moccasins I had never seen; red pumps next to gray ones.

Kneeling beneath her dresses, I smelled my mother's floral cologne as if she had sneaked in beside me. I grabbed the box by its handles and tried to drag it out. Then wrapping my arms around its cool metal sides, I tugged hard at my mother's fortress, harder and harder until the box inched forward.

How much time did I have? Forty-five minutes until Charlie's bus. If my mother hurried at the market, she could be back by then. My heart jumped in my chest. I opened the lid.

A hodgepodge of papers. No file folders or big clasp envelopes. I couldn't pull everything out. How would I get it back in right? Sitting cross-legged on the beige carpeted floor in front of my mother's closet, I thumbed through Charlie's progress reports—in order from preschool through last year—a note from his speech therapist, a letter from one of his teachers. Not jumbled at all, I noticed. A perfect system. His birth certificate had to be there. I found it in front of Charlie's school papers. *Name of father: Louis S. Becker.* I forced all the air from my lungs. Good, not Uncle Ed. But my mother could have lied, I realized. She would have, probably, if Uncle Ed was actually Charlie's father. I'd have to find out some other way, some other time.

What I needed now would be further back, behind Charlie's papers, behind mine. I pushed items forward, ignoring my own life history—school notices, report cards, and swimming certificates from day camp. *Fast, Amy. Faster.* Clothing receipts clipped together. One group for dresses. Another for shoes. My camp list fastened to the sales slip from the store where we'd bought the Takawanda uniform. Household items: a carpet care guide, an air conditioner warranty, a booklet about the refrigerator. Too recent. I didn't need to know how to keep meat fresh. I needed to know who my mother was.

A thick folded paper. I lifted it from behind a pamphlet about the washing machine. *Marriage Certificate*—printed in blue, curlicue letters. It opened like a greeting card, freeing a longer sheet that unfurled. *This is to certify that on the seventh of November in the year 1946, the holy covenant of marriage was entered into at Brooklyn, New York, between the Bridegroom, Louis S. Becker, and his Bride, Sonia Kelman Jonas.*

I stared at my mother's name: Sonia Kelman Jonas. Jonas, a name I had never heard. Did that mean Robin was right about my mother being married before? Married to a man whose last name was Jonas? I drew in a sharp breath. If Robin had gotten that right, maybe there really was another daughter. I slipped the marriage certificate back into the box. That baby in Germany. I had to find her.

The screech of a car made me jump. I raced to the window, though my parents' room didn't face the street. I would never be able to hide my mother's stash quickly enough behind her shield of shoes. Again to the closet. *Breathe, Amy. Breathe.* No sound. Nothing. No one.

The clock on my father's night table told me she couldn't be home yet. More papers. Medical bills and health records. Four bundles: my father's, my mother's, mine, and Charlie's. Camp notices from Uncle Ed. My letters from Takawanda, all folded in their envelopes, a rubber band around them.

More letters behind those. I pulled out an old-fashioned greeting card, red roses on the front. Inside: *Birthday wishes for the one I love.* No date, but my father's handwriting. I was sure of that.

> Dearest Sonia,
>
> I know you will never forget Kurt and Anna, and I will never ask you to. All I ask is that you give me a chance to show how much I love you.

I ran my fingers over the names: Kurt and Anna. Kurt Jonas? My mother's other husband? And Anna. Was she the daughter?

Another card, more flowers on the front:

> Dearest Sonia,
>
> You are right when you say I cannot feel your pain. But you can't go on blaming yourself. You left when you did because you thought that was best. I know you believed Kurt and Anna would meet you in Paris. And I know you think no one will ever love you the way Kurt did. But please, Sonia, let me try.

Time stopped while I read the notes my father had written, the tool he had used to slip into my mother's heart. I couldn't imagine him speaking those words, saying aloud the thoughts he had penned on pretty cards. I couldn't mesh the image of my father then with my picture of him now. How could that be the same man who said, "Sonia, enough Sonia" in an irritated way?

I needed to know more. Why hadn't Kurt met my mother in Paris? And what about Anna? I read until I found the answer:

Dearest Sonia,

Last night when you talked about Anna, I decided we could get married and not have children. I would give up having a family to be with you. But this morning, I knew I was wrong. You keep telling me that Anna was only two when she and Kurt were killed, and that you will never be able to love another child. But now that I know your passion and your strength, I know you will be able to love other children someday. Just as you have learned to love me, you will learn to love the children we will have together.

You are the most beautiful, most exciting woman I have ever met. I want to have children with you. Our children will honor Anna's memory.

I read it again. *Our children will honor Anna's memory.* Again and again until I choked on the truth. I could never be good enough for my mother. No matter how I looked and who my friends were, I would never satisfy her. No matter how many "A"s on my report card, my mother wouldn't want me. She would always want Anna.

A memory ran through my mind. Woolworth's, the day before camp. The cashier punches the wrong key. My mother asks her name. "Anna," she says softly, fearful this customer will tell the manager to fire her. But my mother says only, "I'm sorry, dear," in a voice so soft I don't recognize it.

Now I knew the truth. There was room for only one child in my mother's heart. A baby in Germany. Such a little girl filled all the space my mother had for love the way Charlie filled all the space in our house. I couldn't squeeze in beside Anna. I couldn't replace her—no matter what I did, no matter how I tried.

I stuffed the cards back into the spot from where I had pulled them. Everything in its place, and a place for every thing. Where was my place, I wondered as I shoved my father's notes all the way in so their edges rested perfectly on the bottom of the metal box.

That's when I found the three old photos—two in polished silver frames—buried under papers in the back of the box. I held each to the light, studied them as if I had the power to decipher the past.

The first framed picture gave me Anna: a toddler in a white dress sitting on her mother's lap. My mother, of course, but not the Mom I knew. Anna's mother looks like a movie star, with a smile as wide as the ocean she would cross. Anna rests her tiny hand in her mother's, our mother's. What could this little girl know about the war that would roll over her family like a bulldozer? And how long after this picture was taken until this photo became all my mother had left of her child?

The second picture: a framed portrait of my mother and Kurt, I guessed. He stands next to her, arm around her waist. Her leading man in a dark suit, the kind my father hated wearing. My mother's other life: Mom and Kurt and Anna. That's all she wanted, I thought as I gazed at the man who never made it to Paris. Then I held again the picture of the perfect toddler who claimed my mother's heart.

A third photo curled at scalloped edges, its sepia image creased but not faded. A man all alone, I saw, as handsome as Kurt, but different somehow. Not a stiff handsome but a confident one. A jacket drapes over the man's arm, as if announcing he doesn't need a suit for his image—he's handsome enough without it. I wondered who he was as I flipped the photo over. No inscription, no name. And whom did he remind me of? It hit me with a jolt. That self-assurance. The intensity of his gaze. The photo made me think of a James Dean magazine picture Patsy had shown me. And it made me think of someone else too. Although it wasn't a picture of Uncle Ed, it was his face I saw as I studied the photograph.

Yet even more than the ghosts of that day, what happened next haunts me still. Though I have relived this story a hundred times, searching for ways to erase my guilt, I find only one truth—a simple fact: I didn't hear Charlie's bus. Not then. Not while I looked again at the picture of Anna and my mother. Anna, that child I could never be. I outlined her face, traced her arm to my mother's hand.

I don't know how long the minibus driver waited for someone to come out. How many times did he lean on the horn until I dropped the photo and raced to my brother?

The bus pulled away as Charlie's feet hit the curb. I ran toward him. "Come on, buddy," I yelled, my voice too loud. The metal box. The photographs. I had to put them back before my mother got home. "Come on!" I shouted, grabbing Charlie's hand. "Let's go!" I pulled him toward the house.

"No!" Charlie cried, struggling to free himself. "No!"

I picked him up and ran with him in my arms. "Go upstairs," I ordered when I put Charlie down inside the front door. "I'll be up in a minute." No scream. No answer. I didn't wait for him to move.

Back in my parents' room, I stuffed the pictures into their spot, slammed the lid, pushed the metal box into hiding. The shoes. Brown heels. Navy pumps. What next? White flats, slippers, moccasins. Black shoes. Tan ones.

I turned off the light, closed the closet. No car. No Mom.

"Hey, buddy, I'm sorry," I called, sprinting upstairs. "Charlie, I'm sorry." I raced to his room. Where was he? "Charlie!" Into my room. Empty. "Where are you?" No answer. "I'm sorry, Charlie. Where are you?"

Downstairs again. The front door was open. "Charlie! Charlie!" Outside. Into the street. "Charlie! Where are you?"

Nothing. Then barking. Loud. Ferocious. Zeus, the Sparbers' black Lab. I saw all three in an instant: the dog; Charlie; my mother.

Her car took the corner as Zeus chased Charlie down the block.

"Charlie! Look out, Charlie!"

The screech of tires. A thumping sound: metal on bone. His body flew to the sidewalk.

"CHARLIE!"

Chapter 19

How Was This Possible?

CHARLIE!"
I cried his name, knelt over his body. Such a tiny boy, legs bent like a rag doll's. "No! Charlie!"

Sirens and red lights. Police cars. An ambulance. An officer pulled me up and wrestled me to the other side of the street. "No! Let me go! That's my brother. Charlie!"

"I know, miss. I'm sorry."

Another policeman grabbed my arm. He led me to my mother, sitting on the curb. She was missing a shoe. Her foot rested on a bright green leaf. It's strange what I remember, what I choose to forget. My mother's purse was open, her wallet on the ground next to it. She didn't speak, not even when the officer tried to hand her driver's license back. He placed it under the wallet. My mother didn't notice. Her head stayed down, hands over her mouth.

"Charlie! Charlie!" I called. But my words were a whisper. My voice was dead. Only my tears told me I was alive.

Someone gave me paper cups. Water—for me, for my mother. I saw her from the corner of my eye. She lifted her cup in slow motion, as if trying to figure out what it was. Water dripped on her skirt, the green one from visiting day. The cup fell from her hand. But my mother didn't move.

A policeman stood in front of her. She didn't see the paramedics pack their gear without trying to stuff life back into Charlie. But I did. I watched as if my eyes were no longer part of my body. I saw it from somewhere high above as I looked down on my mother and me, looked down on my brother on the sidewalk across the street.

How was this possible, this movie I watched from the sky? One minute a boy—my brother, my Charlie. Then nothing.

The ambulance moved away. No sirens now. No noise. An officer said something about a tow truck. I think he asked my mother where her husband was.

I don't remember walking down the block, walking home. What I recall is watching myself in Charlie's room, on Charlie's bed. I sat there turning wooden blocks on my lap. I turned them and turned them till my fingers were numb. Rectangle. Square. Triangle. Rectangle. Square. Triangle.

●

We buried him that Sunday. The night before, my father handed me a pill. "To help you sleep, honey. Doctor Stein says you and your mother need to rest." I nodded, though I didn't need help sleeping. Charlie lived in my dreams. All Saturday afternoon I had stayed in my room and slept, pulling Puppy to my face as if I were a little girl again.

I took the pill from Dad's shaking hand. How could he go on as if it mattered if we ate, if we slept? Sure, I'd heard my father crying that whole night after Charlie died. But the next morning, he focused on taking care of my mother and me.

Neither of us had spoken after the accident, except to answer policemen's questions. And even then, we tried to get by with nods and shrugs. It was only when one of the officers forced my mother to tell him about the accident that I heard her voice, soft and flat, the voice of a stranger. She was coming home from the market, my mother said. She had just turned our corner when Charlie ran in front of the car. The dog that chased him raced out of the way, she told the policeman, who asked the same questions the following day, when my parents sat next to each other on the living room sofa. The dog ran to the side, my mother said again, but Charlie didn't.

From my perch on the top step, I listened as my father explained that Charlie and I must have been playing outside when the Sparbers' dog got loose. "Amy is..." my father paused to swallow tears. "She was a wonderful sister. As my wife told you, Amy was taking care of Charlie while she was at the store." Another pause. "Do we really have to go over this again, officer? I'm sure you can see how hard this is for all of us."

"Yes, of course," the policeman said. "I'll be out of your way as soon as I talk to your daughter."

I took the stairs slowly, watching myself put one foot in front of the other. I had killed Charlie. I had done it with my mother. I shared the blame, claimed the lion's share of guilt. But no one knew that. My father had given my excuse. "Yes," I told the officer. "We had just gone outside when Charlie saw Zeus. He took off before I could stop him."

●

No funeral. Just a burial with a rabbi. The Hebrew prayers sounded like crying. Uncle Ed, Aunt Helen, and Robin stood on one side of the grave, but I didn't look at them. My father held on to my mother and me on the other side of the hole in the ground. He let go only to toss dirt onto the small casket and to hand the shovel to my mother, her face carved of stone. She barely scooped up anything, then passed the shovel to me. I saw myself drizzle earth onto Charlie's coffin. "I love you, buddy." My lips moved, but there was no sound.

After the burial, the world rolled on and left us behind. Each day I took a block from Charlie's room and carried it to mine, where I'd cling to sleep. I slept to see Charlie in my dreams, and I slept to avoid my parents. We didn't talk about the accident. We didn't talk about anything—just spun cocoons of grief and disappeared inside them.

I didn't reply to the note from Erin or the sympathy card from Donnie. How had they found out? Had Uncle Ed or Aunt Helen called them?

"You should write back to Erin," my father told me. "Or you could call and make a date. I'll drive you to visit her." I didn't want to explain why I couldn't see Erin. I hadn't told my

217

father—hadn't told anyone—that Charlie would be alive if I hadn't gone to camp. The logic was simple: Without camp, I wouldn't have been tempted to invade my mother's past. And Charlie would still be here. So how could I visit Erin and talk about Rory, sing silly camp songs, and smile at Andy's name? I didn't even answer Andy's letter, which came shortly after school started.

Tenth grade. Kids avoided me as if death were contagious. And if girls caught my eye, the pity in theirs made me eager to run. I stopped riding the school bus. The noise was too loud; the life, too much. So I walked every day by myself. One morning Danielle's mother pulled up and offered me a ride. But I didn't take it. Even in the cold, I wanted to walk. I needed to feel my feet slap the pavement. I needed to remember my body was alive.

My mother didn't seem to care if I grabbed a coat when the weather turned cold. She didn't say a word about what I wore or how I fixed my hair or if I ate the wrong things. She no longer noticed if I made my bed or made the honor roll.

But I noticed her. She stopped plumping pillows on the sofa. Even when people came to visit—neighbors stopping by with casseroles; Charlie's speech therapist and two of his teachers from The Woodland Center—my mother didn't care if I replaced the toilet paper, if the kitchen floor looked waxed, if her shoes matched her outfit. Sometimes she just shuffled around in a bathrobe and slippers, as if she'd forgotten to get dressed.

My father noticed too. One night when we sat at the kitchen table and tried to ignore Charlie's place, Dad told us the accounting firm he worked for had opened a small office in New Haven. They needed one more man there, he said. So my father had volunteered. We were moving to Connecticut. "A new start," he explained, tears shining in his eyes. "And for God's sake, we need it."

"Okay," I said, because, really, what difference did it make where I lived?

Without a word, my mother got up to clear the pizza from the table.

"Sonia, a new start, Sonia," my father said again. He stood to hug her. I watched my mother stiffen, the way she had with Uncle Ed. But this time, I understood why she froze. If my mother would let anyone in — even her husband — she might feel. And if she felt, she might finally break.

No outer world in; no inner world out. Everything in its place, including our grief.

●

We moved to Connecticut in March, to a two-bedroom house with a postage-stamp lawn. No need for a third bed-room when no one would fill it. No use for a yard when no one would play there. It didn't matter that my new room was small. I'd packed only my clothes, a few letters I'd saved, and some photographs — a thin album of pictures I had snapped with Charlie's camera and a few loose photos in an envelope. Before we moved, Erin sent me the picture she had taken on visiting day: Charlie and me at the camp-craft area. I put it in the envelope, along with the photo of Charlie standing by the tower we'd built on the morning I left for camp.

Again my father urged me to call Erin. "I know you'd like to thank her for the picture," he said, suggesting I might want to talk to her and hinting that I should. But after Charlie died, I started thinking that my father always believed he knew what I wanted, just like when he told us about Takawanda. "Of course you want to go to camp," he had said. "Who wouldn't want eight weeks by a lake in Maine?"

I don't, I had tried to tell him. But my father hadn't listened. If he would have heard me and not sent me to Takawanda, then Robin might never have teased me about my mother, and I wouldn't have pulled out that stupid metal box. And then Charlie would still be alive. So even though my mother and I had killed him, my father shared the blame. He just didn't know it—didn't know much of anything, I decided after Charlie died.

I stopped agreeing with everything my father said, and I didn't call Erin. The sound of her voice would have wormed through my heart. And if I felt, then I too might break. So I just sent a note, formal and stiff, and convinced myself that Mrs. Hollander would read the missing words. I counted on her to tell Erin that part of me had died with Charlie: the part that welcomed an arm on my shoulder; the part that knew how to love. Mrs. Hollander would realize I had shut myself down. She'd explain that to Erin, I wanted to believe. And then Erin would know why I couldn't be her friend. Couldn't be anyone's friend, in fact. Just *being* was hard enough.

I had packed one more thing for the new house: Charlie's wooden blocks, safe in a carton with my name on it. My father didn't ask where they were when he emptied Charlie's room. Yet he had to see the naked shelves, where the rectangles, squares, and triangles belonged. But my father didn't need an accounting of items, and my mother wouldn't ask for one now. The requirement of perfection no longer ruled our lives.

Charlie's blocks weren't the only things missing from their assigned places. The week before we moved, I tucked my porcelain dogs and Russian dolls into a box marked "Salvation Army." Then I threw Puppy into the trash.

●

My new school was not very different from my old: the same types of kids and the same kinds of cliques. I didn't worry about fitting in, didn't want to, in fact. Easier to keep to myself. Easier not to get close, not to let anyone ask if I had brothers or sisters, where we moved from and why. Easier to be like my mother, I found. Like mother, like daughter, we twinned in our grief.

My father tried to keep us going. On his way home from work, he'd buy something for dinner. We ate at our new kitchen table—barely large enough for three chairs. My father might have thought our sorrow would shrink if we didn't see an empty seat. But in this little space, our pain began to swell. And the longer we didn't speak of Charlie, the more his presence grew. After a while, his ghost filled the new house. There was no room for outsiders.

It didn't matter, though. We had no friends, no visitors— except Uncle Ed and Aunt Helen. They came to see us one Sunday about a month after we moved. My father greeted them outside, then ushered them into the living room, where my mother and I positioned ourselves because my father had reminded us they were family after all.

"Robin sends her love," Uncle Ed said. He opened his arms to my mother, who stepped back, next to me. My uncle's arms fell to his sides as he studied her, a statue in the beige dress that used to gently hug her body. Now it billowed like a poor hand-me-down.

Uncle Ed brushed his palms through his hair. "What I was saying is Robin's sorry she couldn't come with us. You know how teenagers are," he went on with a wink. "So many friends. So busy on the weekends."

"Well anyhoodle," Aunt Helen said, "it's nice to see you. And what a cute little place you've got here."

My mother and I escaped to the kitchen. I opened the box of "company cookies" my mother kept, just in case. She put on the coffee. I remember watching her in that too-big dress, a slip peeking out from the bottom. Sonia Becker, not perfect anymore.

But what I remember most about the year after Charlie died is the silence. It made the air too dense to breathe. And something else too: By the end of the school year, all my mother's clothes were too big. My father wanted to take her shopping. "What do I need clothes for?" She asked. Six words. The longest sentence I had heard my mother speak in a while.

Sometime after that, my father called the doctor. And sometime later, the cancer was confirmed.

I tried not to sleep that night, tried to focus on the sounds from my parents' room. Crying—both of them—for what seemed too long. I was sorry I'd thrown Puppy away. I wanted to clutch my stuffed animal, to hold childhood one last time. I pulled myself into a ball and listened to my parents' hushed voices, listened far into the night until sleep finally grabbed me. And when I awoke and padded to the bathroom, I heard something I didn't remember ever having heard before: the sighs and moans and whispers of my mother and father loving each other.

Chapter 20

Tell Me What Happened

My mother started talking to me the next day. It was as if she had chosen, finally, to strip off her armor. As suddenly as that, she let the past out and let me slip in.

I would come home from school, junior year, and prop the pillows under her head. My mother lay on the sofa in the living room. The pink robe my father had bought swirled around her tiny frame, which shrunk even more with each treatment.

My mother would greet me with a smile, lips barely curled. I knew she was trying to say she was sorry. Sorry she locked me out of her life. Sorry she never hugged me. She didn't say those words, of course, but her apology warmed me all the same.

Its form was a story, one I'd hungered to hear. Each day, a snippet of her life. She talked until her eyes closed, and I panicked she was gone. Strange, how I used to pray for her death. Now I clung to her life.

Sometimes after a few minutes, my mother would open her eyes and talk again. And sometimes she would wait for me to ask what she was thinking about. It was hard to ask anything at first. All those years of not questioning, a habit tough to break. But we were different now. My mother wanted me to ask, and she needed to keep talking.

"I'm thinking about when I was young," she whispered. I saw my mother in the word pictures she finally drew for me, with her accent that didn't bother me anymore. Through her stories, I met my mother's family. Two brothers: one who never got out of Germany and one, Walter, who made it to Paris, then Auschwitz. They were older than she was, my mother told me. They called her a pest. But when her brothers studied English in school and ran around the house yelling "all right, all right, all right," her father said *they* were the pesky ones.

My mother smiled when she spoke of her father, a language professor, I found out. He talked to my mother mostly in French. He took her—just her, not her brothers—to his office in the city. Through my mother's eyes, I saw the University of Bonn, the big building where her father worked. Polished doorknobs. Shiny floors. "It's strange, what I remember," my mother said, as I pulled my chair closer, anxious to catch every word.

"Tell me what happened, Mom." She worked at another smile. A smile for her memories. A smile now, I believed, for me.

I sat on the edge of the chair and waited, desperate for another story, another glimpse. Slivers and fragments. Pieces of my mother's life. I gobbled them and wanted more. And the more she talked, the more I recalled the clues, those random scraps I'd discarded through the years.

Her own mother died when she was only five, my mother said. I remembered: My father had told me when I'd asked about my grandparents. But I hadn't heard the rest of the story, how my mother's father remarried a couple of years later. How after the stepmother had her own son, she nearly ignored my mother and her brothers.

"My best friend was Elsa," my mother whispered one day as I placed a blanket over her, leaning in for her words. "She lived next door. She wasn't Jewish. Her mother baked spicy little cookies with sugar powder on them. *Pfeffernüsse*. Little cookie balls. Elsa's mother baked them at Christmas."

I wanted more about Elsa—a scene I could see. But it wasn't Elsa my mother wanted to talk about. It was Elsa's older brother, Otto. Funny, smart, and handsome, my mother told me. A popular boy. Everyone liked him. "When I was a teenager," she said, "just a little older than you are, Otto began calling on me. We went for walks. Sometimes we went to the city, to a café." My mother paused for a moment, perhaps replaying a memory. "We had a good time," she went on. "Otto made me laugh."

My mother laughing. A sound I had never heard. "Was Otto your boyfriend?" I asked, choking on the words, though I didn't imagine my mother would mind that question now. How different from the mother who had raised me. Yet though we weren't the same people, asking her about a boyfriend sent a tingle through me. But still, I wanted to know. I wanted to see her as a teenager. Was she pretty then, I wondered. As pretty as she was in the photos I had found? And popular? And smart?

"Yes, Otto was my boyfriend," she answered without bitterness or anger. So it was Otto, I knew, whose picture I had studied. That third photo: the man who reminded me of Uncle Ed. "But we had a hard time," my mother told me. "First with Elsa, and then with... with everything that happened."

"What?" I pulled the chair right up to the sofa, and for the very first time, I reached for my mother's hand.

It took days for her to tell me the whole story. At first, she said, the biggest problem was Elsa. Elsa was jealous. She didn't like my mother spending so much time with her brother. But that was nothing compared with what happened later. "Elsa stopped saying hello when we passed in the street," my mother said, "like she didn't even recognize me. And her parents told Otto he had to stop seeing me. No more mixing with Jews, they said. *Verboten.*"

The next year my mother met Kurt. Kurt Jonas, she told me. His family owned a clothing store in Bonn. And despite the depression that hit Germany hard, Kurt's family stayed in business.

"Another boyfriend? Did you love him, Mom? Like you loved Otto?"

"Yes." My mother sighed. "It was different. But yes, I loved him very much. And my father was so happy when Kurt asked me to marry him. A Jewish boy from a good family—educated, successful." She stopped for a moment to catch her breath. "In those days, we had to believe our lives in Germany would get better, even though most of us knew things were getting worse. And what could be better than getting married?"

I faked surprise at her having been married to someone other than my father. But it didn't matter. My mother didn't see my reaction as she talked about Kurt. And I couldn't say that I already knew. I couldn't tell her Robin had shared her secrets. I couldn't admit I had broken into her metal box. I didn't think I was ready to talk about Charlie.

My mother and Kurt had a good marriage, she said, though things in Germany did get worse, much worse. Her father urged them to leave the country. He wanted the whole family to go. But his wife wouldn't hear of it. "This is our home," the stepmother said. "We're all Germans, after all. This Hitler business will end soon."

My mother took a shallow breath. Then very slowly: "Amy, there's something else. Something you should know."

I curled my fingers around the edge of my seat, squeezed the dark green velveteen fabric. I knew what she was about to tell me. I leaned forward to catch every word.

"Kurt and I had a baby. Anna." Tears filled her whispered words. "I'm sorry I never told you. But I...I couldn't talk about her." I pulled closer and took my mother's hand again.

Anna was only two, she said, when Kurt tried to get documents for the three of them to go to France. My mother's brother Walter was already in Paris. He rented a room there from an artist who needed income more than studio space. If my mother could get to Paris, she figured, she'd be able to stay with Walter for a little while, just long enough to find a job and an apartment. Her command of French, along with a bribe, would get her working papers. But there would be no working papers for Kurt, my mother told me. Not for a German Jewish businessman who didn't speak French. Yet for my mother, there was a chance of a job and temporary lodging. Her brother's landlady might let her in, she believed, if unencumbered by a husband and child.

Kurt pleaded for the three of them to go together.

"But think about Anna," my mother said. "At least here she still has a place to sleep. Where would the three of us go in France without jobs, without a place to stay? If I go alone to Paris, Walter will be able to help me."

My mother was scared to go by herself. Terrified, she told me. And leaving Anna was the hardest thing she ever did. But it was Anna she was thinking of when she begged Kurt to let her go first. "Anna's just a baby. She needs food and a bed. A hungry, crying child will only bring attention. But if I go ahead, I can find us a safe place to live. And then you'll bring Anna."

It was Otto who got my mother out. Otto—a good man, she said. He hadn't forgotten her, even after she married Kurt.

Otto had friends in the government, acquaintances at the embassies. He had always been popular, my mother reminded me. Otto would get the papers for her and for Kurt and Anna. Yet though he could do that, he couldn't control the cost. His friends in high places worked slowly. It took money—lots of money—to grease the wheels.

By the fall of 1938, Kurt's family sold what they could. Then Otto went to work. Though all Jewish passports had been annulled, emigration permits were available—expedited for a price, of course. And the quota for entry to France could be manipulated if you knew the right people, the people Otto knew.

He got documents for my mother and for Kurt and Anna. "Please," Kurt tried again. "We must go together."

"But we haven't much more money, and no place for all of us in Paris," my mother reminded him. "I have to go first. I have to find a safe place for Anna. And then you'll come. Just a week or two. That's all I need."

November 8, 1938. My mother kissed her husband and her little girl, then blazed the trail she believed they would follow.

"And what happened to Anna?" I asked. I didn't want to hear, but I needed to know.

"The next night, the storm troopers came. *Kristallnacht.* Night of Broken Glass."

It took time for my mother to find out what happened that night, but eventually she did. She heard and she imagined. And she never forgave herself for having left without her child.

Kurt would have carried Anna to the back room when the commotion started, my mother thought. He might have wrapped her in blankets and laid her down gently, her doll in hand.

Perhaps Anna was sleeping when the storm troopers arrived. Kurt might have met them at the door. He would have told them his wife and daughter were away. "There's no one else here," Kurt probably said as they pulled him outside and sent the search party in.

But then Anna cried out, my mother believed. The way she pictured it, a Nazi yelled "Who is this?" as he dragged Anna onto the street. "Your daughter? The one who's gone? *Nicht hier?*"

While the storm troopers murdered Kurt, my mother imagined, members of the Hitler Youth kicked Anna like a soccer ball. My mother hoped Kurt had died first. She hoped he wasn't forced to watch their little girl suffer.

This story hit me hard. I cried for Kurt. I cried for Anna. Mostly, though, I cried for my mother.

"That's what I see when I close my eyes," she said. "Boys kicking Anna like a ball. I never should have left her. We all would have gotten out if I had listened to Kurt. We could have left together, and somehow we would have managed."

"You did what you thought you had to, Mom." I brushed away tears—hers and my own. "You tried to do the right thing to make her life better."

We stayed quiet for a while. Then my mother said, "I'm sorry, Amy. I should have told you. But people don't always do the right thing, even when they think they are. And somehow we just have to forgive them, forgive ourselves."

I tried to swallow, but sorrow and guilt filled my throat. It was time to tell her about the metal box. It was time to tell her that I, not she, had killed Charlie. My mother had suffered so much, so long. I couldn't let her carry the blame for Charlie's death too.

"But it all worked out all right," she went on before I found my words. "All right. All right. All right." My mother's lips trembled. Then a tiny smile. "I came here and met your father. And he was good to me. And I had you...and Charlie."

"Mom, there's something I have to tell you. The metal box..."

"I know." Her eyes closed. She needed to sleep, or wanted to sleep. Maybe in her dreams my mother saw Anna the way I saw Charlie in mine.

"But I have to tell you, Mom. About Charlie. About the accident."

"I know, Amy," she whispered. "I know what happened that day. We don't have to talk about it."

I exhaled as if I'd been holding my breath for a very long time. So my mother knew the truth after all. I must have left clues: shoes out of order, papers out of place. My mother knew I had breached her privacy. And she knew the price I had already paid.

"I didn't tell anyone, not even your father," my mother said. "Certain things are just too hard to talk about. Certain things are meant to stay private."

My mother stretched out her arm. I wove my fingers with hers. *I am Sonia's daughter*, I said to myself. *Sonia Kelman Jonas Becker.*

I thought about Anna—Anna and Kurt and Mom—as my mother squeezed my hand gently, very gently. And then she did the most amazing thing. My mother said she loved me.

Chapter 21

Pick Up the Pieces

Now I lie awake at night and pray Mom's cancer's gone for good. The doctors say it might be.

I picture her at my graduation tomorrow: Mom in her new light blue dress, so much better looking than the other mothers. Dad will escort her to one of those folding chairs in front of the bleachers. She will sit tall, her back perfectly straight again, and wait for me to walk by in my cap and gown. My mother will be smiling. And so will I.

●

Now I know my mother's story, and now I understand. My mother could never have bounced me on her knee. That was reserved for Anna's ghost, the one that slipped into the hospital the day I was born. There was no room for outsiders, no room for hopes and dreams. All my mother had were her memories, the stories she eventually gifted to me. I treasure those images of my mother before her world broke apart. How had she managed to pick up the pieces? What courage, to cobble splinters into a whole new life. So I forgive her for not being able to love me the way I needed her to. Forgave her, in fact, last year as I watched her fight to live.

•

"Your mother is so proud of you, Amy," my father told me earlier this evening, while Mom was washing up for bed. Dad had come into my room to congratulate me, for the tenth time, on the scholarship to NYU and on my English award.

"Dad, it's just high school. It's not like I'm graduating summa cum laude from college or anything."

"But it's still a big accomplishment, honey. I'm just so glad your mother's here to see this."

We stayed silent for a moment, both of us probably thinking about Mom—about Charlie too, I was sure. My father and I had never spoken of Charlie's accident. I hadn't told him of my guilt. It was my mother I had tried to tell. It was my mother whose burden I had wanted to lighten.

"You know," Dad went on, "the very first time I saw your mother, I thought she was the most beautiful woman I'd ever seen. And not a day has gone by when I haven't thought I'm the luckiest man in the world. No one can hold a candle to her, Ame. And you? Well…you look more and more like your mother each day."

I'd seen it too lately: my mother's face looking back from the mirror.

"Dad, I need to tell you something."

"Sure, honey. What is it?"

I shut my eyes and focused on breathing. In. Out. In. Out. No outer world in; no inner world out. "Certain things are just too hard to talk about," my mother had told me.

Hard, yes. But on this night before graduation, I needed to talk about Charlie, to nudge his ghost off my chest. Scoot, scoot, skedaddle. It was time to tell the truth.

Charlie and Takawanda knotted in my thoughts. "Dad," I said, my voice catching, "why'd you make me go to camp?"

In my mind, Rory raced into the dining hall. She slammed the door to shut me out.

I wanted to tell my father what had happened that summer. But all I could say was, "It was awful. Just because Uncle Ed bought Takawanda, I shouldn't have had to go. He didn't have a clue about what really went on there. I'm glad he doesn't own it anymore."

"You know, honey, I thought I was doing the right thing then. A whole summer by a lake in Maine. A chance to be on your own for a while without worrying about your brother."

"But if you wouldn't have sent me, then Charlie wouldn't have died."

"What are you saying?"

"I never told you how Robin teased me and what she said about Mom." My voice became a whisper. "And I never told you about the accident."

My father sat next to me on the bed. He put his arm around me. "I think I know what happened."

"But Mom said she didn't tell you."

"She didn't. She never said a word. No one keeps secrets better than your mother."

What secrets was he talking about? My mother and her past? Mom and Uncle Ed? Did my father know about that, I wondered for a moment, though I realized it didn't matter anymore. Even when my mother welcomed questions, I knew not to ask about my uncle. "Certain things are meant to stay private," Mom had whispered. Her affair with Uncle Ed was one of those things.

"But if Mom didn't tell you about Charlie, about the accident, then how do you know?"

"It wasn't hard to figure out, Ame. When I thought about it, I realized you and Charlie couldn't have been playing together outside when that dog came, because if you were there when Charlie started running, you surely would have caught him."

Tears came from a place so deep I couldn't stop them—nor could I stop the questions that rushed from my mouth. "Why didn't you say anything? Why didn't we ever talk about this?"

My father pulled me to my feet and hugged me tight. "I assumed you'd talk about Charlie when you were ready."

My words rolled out with sobs. "I killed him, Dad. I killed Charlie when I let him wander away. If I hadn't been snooping in Mom's things, Charlie wouldn't have taken off. And he wouldn't have died, Dad. He wouldn't be dead."

My father held me for a long time. "Amy," he finally said, his voice shaky and soft. "Amy, I'm so very sorry. I should have talked to you about this long ago. I hope you can forgive me. Forgive me for not talking about Charlie. Forgive me for sending you to Takawanda. But more important, honey—so much more important—I hope that, someday, you'll forgive yourself."

I heard my mother's voice as if she, not my father, embraced me. *People don't always do the right thing, even when they think they are. And somehow we just have to forgive them, forgive ourselves.*

"Dad," I said, before my courage faded, "why didn't you ever tell me about Mom? Why didn't we talk about her life in Germany? And why didn't I know about Anna?"

My father took a step back and rested his hands on my shoulders. "Your mother's tried so hard to shut out the past. It's just so painful for her. And when you were born, she made me promise I wouldn't talk about it either. She saw you as a fresh start, Ame. And she wanted to forget. She needed to forget. But she just can't. She can't ever forget."

"She told me, Dad. When she was really sick, she told me about Anna."

"It was her story to tell, honey, not mine. I've always respected her privacy. I just love her so much."

I looked up and saw a tear run down my father's cheek. "It's okay, Dad. I understand."

My father wrapped me in his arms again. I breathed in his aftershave, that woodsy scent of my childhood. "Your mother has spent her whole life feeling guilty about Anna—so guilty she couldn't even talk about her. I'm glad you can talk about Charlie now. You were a wonderful sister to him. He was so lucky to have you. So please, honey, please don't repeat your mother's mistake. You've got your whole life in front of you. Don't waste it feeling guilty. All your mother and I want is for you to be happy."

•

Sometimes in my dreams, Charlie gives me lovely things: building blocks and endless hugs.

And sometimes I dream about Takawanda: Rory at the social, Erin in the boathouse, Andy at the bus.

•

Maybe in college I'll face other Rorys. I know I'll stand tall and speak up without fear.

I wonder what happened to her after that summer. Did her father continue to abuse her? Erin wasn't sure he ever really did. But if it were true, then I hope he finally stopped.

The few times I saw cousin Robin after camp, we didn't talk about Rory. And my father quit talking about Uncle Ed all the time. Dad's angry with him, I know, because Uncle Ed rarely called when Mom was sick.

•

Maybe in college I'll meet other Erins. I want to stay true, to be a better friend than I was to Erin Hollander.

Last week, while shopping with new friends, I bought three cards. *It's been a long time*, they say on the front. And inside: *Better late than never.* I sent them off this morning, with notes of apology. I don't expect Erin and Donnie and Andy to write back. But they each deserve an explanation and long overdue thanks.

●

Lately in my dreams, Erin and I walk on a path through the pines—my arm around her waist, her arm around mine. We walk and we walk. And the path doesn't end. And we don't look for Rory. We don't even talk. And when I wake up, I know I've been smiling.

Mostly, though, I dream about my mother. I picture her stories. I see myself sitting next to her. She squeezes my hand. She tells me she loves me.

Yes, Dad is right: My mother is proud.

College, here I come.

A Note from the Author

Dear Reader,

I hope you enjoyed *Camp*, and that it was hard for you to put it down. Sometimes when I read a novel that's hard for *me* to put down, I wonder if the main character resembles the author and how much of the story actually happened in real life. So in case *you're* wondering, I thought I'd tell you a little about myself and some of the similarities and differences between me and Amy Becker.

Unlike Amy, I loved sleepaway camp. I could hardly wait for summer so I could go back to Camp Truda for Girls in Maine. Truda was owned by my uncle, as the fictional Takawanda is owned by Amy's uncle. But *my* uncle ran a terrific camp (as many camps are), where the rules were strictly enforced—and I was scared to break them. I did, however, once sneak out with my friends to trek through the woods to the nearest boys camp. And much to my distress, my uncle did report that to my father.

Takawanda looks just like I remember Truda. That's one of their few similarities. Both camps—the one I created and the one in my memory—are hauntingly beautiful. Years before I wrote this novel, I knew that a sleepaway camp would be the perfect setting for a coming-of-age story.

Just as camp was the most comfortable place for me, coming-of-age novels were the most comfortable books for me—and they still are. I think some part of me is stuck in the teenage years. Psychologists would probably say I have "unresolved issues." But I think I'm stuck here because I've always been involved with teenagers—as a camp counselor, a recreation leader, a special education teacher, a reading teacher, a writers' workshop facilitator, a judge for young authors' contests, and as a public school district chairperson for English language arts.

Fortunately my own teen years weren't bad—not at all like Amy Becker's. But still, there were moments that made me shudder: like when my parents brought fruit instead of junk food on visiting day. That memory found its way into *Camp*.

Like Amy's mother, my mother was an immigrant who rarely spoke about her life in Germany. In fact, one of the very few things I remember her telling me was that in Germany no one brought their dogs inside. That made it to the pages of *Camp* too.

Many years ago one of my cousins, who is not at all like Amy's cousin Robin, told me something about my mother's past that surprised me. How did my cousin know more about my mother than I did? But my parents didn't want to discuss it. So I gave Amy the gift of finally knowing *her* mother.

I hope you'll share *Camp* with *your* mother—and with your friends and teachers as well. I hope, too, that you'll share your thoughts about *Camp* with me. Please visit my website at authorelainewolf.com.

Wishing you a happy life,
Elaine Wolf

Acknowledgments

A huge shout-out to those who read early drafts of this story and to those who cheered from the sidelines:

Ruth Thaler, whose unwavering support, nurturing, and friendship kept me writing; Lou Stanek and Jill Davis, whose knowledge and guidance made this a better book; Bee Cullinan and Mary Tahan, whose encouragement sustained me; Howard Rosenberg, Bill Rosenberg, Bernie Rosenberg, Alice Moss, Ali Moss, Roselle and Bernie Wolf, Donna and Frank Miller-Small, Kathy Greenstein, Florence Kopit, Bea Nasaw, Ileanna Pappas, Sandy Bernstein, Cara Greene, Hortense Gray, Arlette Sanders, my writing and book groups, and my Long Island and Northampton friends, whose belief that they'd see *Camp* on the shelves (or on e-readers) guaranteed I wouldn't give up.

Thunderous applause for my publishing team:

Jennifer Lyons, my agent, whose dedication and advocacy led her to find the perfect home for this book; Julie Matysik, my editor, whose hard work, intelligence, and grace ensured a joyful publishing experience; Tony Lyons, my publisher, and his Skyhorse team — especially Brian Peterson and Yvette Grant, whose commitment to this book was exceptional.

And a million hugs to my family:

Adam and Sumana Wolf, and Judy Wolf and Justin David, my remarkable children, whose love and confidence empowered me to fly; Ira Wolf, my amazing husband and greatest champion, whose patience, understanding, and generous spirit enabled me to soar. Without him, there would be no book.

Heartfelt thanks to you all.

Discussion Questions for Camp

1. The most realistic characters in novels evoke our sympathy at times and our lack of sympathy at other times. When and why do you have sympathy for Amy? And when, if ever, don't you have sympathy for her? Using this framework, discuss Amy's mother, her father, and Rory as characters for whom you feel sympathy at some times and a lack of sympathy at others.

2. There are many interesting relationships in *Camp*. Discuss the relationship between Amy and her mother; the relationship between Amy and her brother, Charlie; Amy and her cousin, Robin; Amy's father and his brother, Uncle Ed; and Amy's mother and Uncle Ed.

3. Another interesting relationship is the one between Amy's mother and father. Why do you think Amy's father doesn't stand up to her mother? Is Amy's father a good father? Why or why not?

4. Why does Amy say she hates her mother? Why does her mother's accent bother Amy so much? Do you think children of immigrants often feel embarrassed by their parents? If so, why?

5. Even though Amy says she hates her mother, she still seeks her mother's approval. She wants her mother to think that she's popular, smart, and pretty. Why?

6. Early in the novel, Amy wonders why her mother needs everything to be done in a particular way. "But why this requirement of perfection," Amy asks herself, "those stupid rules that governed our lives?" Why do you think Amy's mother imposes this requirement of perfection? What function do her rules serve for her? And why is Amy's mother obsessed with appearances?

7. The characters in *Camp* make many choices. What motivates the choices that Amy, her mother, her father, Rory, Erin, Uncle Ed, and Patsy make? While reading, how did you feel about their choices? After reading, do you have new insights about the choices they make?

8. Why does Amy lie in her letters? Why doesn't she tell anyone what's really happening at Camp Takawanda? What do you think could have or would have happened had Amy told the truth?

9. At the beginning of the camp season, when Rory threatens Amy with a "special introduction" to the kitchen boys, Amy can't find her voice. Why can't she talk back to Rory? What do you think you might have done if you were Amy? What might you have done if you were one of the other campers?

10. Critics call *Camp* a multi-layered story with many themes. Some say it's a novel about trying to fit in; others say it's about secrets; still others write that it's mainly about bullying. What do you think are the main themes of *Camp*?

11. *Camp* has been described as "a story about the collateral damage of secrets." Which characters hold secrets? What purposes do secrets serve for these characters? What harm is caused by the secrets in this novel?

12. In interviews, the author defines bullying as "aggressive behavior that's hurtful, intentional, threatening, and persistent." With this definition in mind, who are the bullies in *Camp*? How do they elicit fear and compliance? How do they maintain their power?

13. Why does Rory choose a new target after visiting day? What does that tell us about bullies? Why do you think Amy's cousin, Robin, sides with Rory?

14. Sometimes the adults who are supposed to keep kids safe fail in their responsibilities. Could Nancy, the head counselor, have stopped the bullying? Should Clarence, who is in charge of the kitchen, have intervened? Is Uncle Ed also to blame? Why doesn't he take action?

15. Do you think Erin is a good friend to Amy? Why or why not? What are the characteristics of a good friend?

16. There are several recurring sayings or expressions in this story—"everything in its place, and a place for every thing," for example. What are some other repeated sayings? How do they add to your reading of *Camp*?

17. Discuss the symbolism of Amy's mother's metal box, of her perfectly fluffed pillows, and of Amy's Russian nesting dolls.

18. *Camp* is often called a coming-of-age novel. By the time Amy leaves Camp Takawanda, she is quite different from how she is when she arrives. What lessons does Amy learn at camp? What does Amy want at the beginning of

the summer? What does she want at the end? Does she get what she wants? If so, what price does she pay to attain it?

19. At the end of *Camp*, we learn about Amy's mother's history. Does her background justify the way in which she treats her children? Do you feel differently about Amy's mother after you know her story? Toward the beginning of *Camp*, Amy wonders: "Why couldn't my mother just love us?" What is the answer to that question? And how does Amy come to forgive her mother?

20. There are two epigraphs at the beginning of the novel. One is attributed to William Faulkner: "The past is never dead. It's not even past." The other is from Anne Michaels: "My parents' past is mine molecularly." Discuss these quotes as they relate to *Camp*.

A Conversation with Elaine Wolf

Q: What inspires your writing? And, specifically, what inspired you to write *Camp*?

A: In general, my novels are informed by my work as a middle school and high school teacher. I love teenagers, and I'm troubled by some school and camp cultures in which our teens learn to navigate their worlds. I'm angry that the adults we charge with keeping our children safe sometimes turn their backs on the victims and ignore the bullies. And, as a parent and grandparent, I'm haunted by the knowledge that danger can be present when we're not around to protect our children—and, sometimes, even when we are.

A confluence of thoughts brought me to *Camp*. Many years before I wrote this book, my son told me of an incident that happened when he was a camper. His group was on an overnight camping trip and the counselors took off at night, leaving the boys all alone in the middle of nowhere. My son admitted he had been frightened. And I became increasingly aware of the fact that the adults we rely on to keep our children safe sometimes fall short.

Also, when thinking about the story that became *Camp*, I thought about my mother, who died many years earlier. She was a German immigrant who lost family in the concentration camps. I miss her terribly, and as I get older, I'm increasingly sad that I don't know her full story. Like Sonia in *Camp*, my mother rarely talked about her life in Germany.

While my mother was dying, I re-read Robert Cormier's *The Moustache*. There's a transformational line in that story: "My parents exist outside of their relationship with me." I thought about that a lot as I said goodbye to my mother. Who was she outside of her relationship with my siblings and me? Who, really, was this woman I knew only as Mom? In *Camp*, Amy's mother holds a dark secret from her past. And Amy doesn't find out who her mother really is, what her life was like outside of her role as Amy's mother, until the very end of the book. That's a gift I decided to give to Amy: the treasure of knowing her mother's story.

Lastly, I've always been moved by the courage of immigrants, who must cobble together splinters of the past to create new lives. I often think about the trickle-down impact of war on displaced people and future generations.

In *Camp*, Amy's mother's past significantly affects her relationship with Amy.

Q: Relationships are really important in *Camp*, especially Amy's relationship with her brother. How did you create their very special bond?

A: Here's what I knew about Amy before I started writing *Camp*: She's a "big sister" and a "good girl" who desperately wants her mother's approval and who doesn't want to go away to summer camp. I don't know why, but the voices of some of the children with whom I had worked when I was a special education teacher started screaming in my mind when I wrote one of the opening scenes of the book, in which Amy and her family are at the dinner table and her father announces that Amy will be going to sleep-away camp. I pictured a young boy who had been my student in a summer program for children with special needs more than forty years ago. His name was Charlie, and he was a beautiful little boy who was prone to tantrums.

Charlie's first tantrum in *Camp*, and the way in which Amy and her parents respond, showed me so much about Charlie, the family relationships, and the very special bond between Amy and Charlie. Their relationship grew organically from that early scene, and it became a driving force in the book.

Q: How did you create the struggle between Amy and her mother?

A: As I said, Amy's primary need or want is her mother's approval. So, creating a struggle between Amy and her mother—a struggle that rings true—was crucial. In imagining Sonia, I thought a lot about my own mother. As I told you, my mother, like Sonia, was an immigrant who rarely spoke about her life in Germany. So, in portraying Amy's mother, I took some of my own mother's characteristics—her wall of privacy, her courage, her perfectionism, her beauty—and I bumped them up tenfold to make them sizzle and to make them the sharp edges against which Amy constantly crashes. Given these two characters, the struggle was always present as I wrote *Camp*. Creating characters with these needs, wants, and personalities allowed the struggle between Amy and her mother to build on itself.

Q: How did you create Rory?

A: While I was writing the scene about Amy on the bus heading to Camp Takawanda for Girls, Rory's voice just barged into my head. It was so loud in my mind. So, the truth is, I just tried to get out of my own way and let the characters dictate the story. As soon as I had a timid first-time camper, Amy, and an alpha girl "queen of mean," Rory, *Camp* really took off.

I don't know why, but I have such fun writing mean girls! Maybe it's because I was always a "good girl" and writing "mean" gives me a chance to explode on the page.

Q: What led you to the plot points concerning Charlie?

A: Although I love dogs, I was terrified of them when I was very young. I decided to give that fear to Charlie, which led to the scene on visiting day. As I was writing the book, I knew that Charlie's fear of dogs would be important to the story. Otherwise, I wouldn't have given him that fear.

I also knew from the beginning that Amy's mother would have to pay a price for her privacy, and that Amy would pay a price for invading it. In fact, the working title of the manuscript was *The Price of Privacy*. I knew, too, that Charlie's fear of dogs and Amy's invading her mother's privacy would come together in a dramatic moment.

Q: Why did you set *Camp* in the 1960s?

A: One of the editors to whom my agent submitted *Camp* asked if I would change the story to have it take place in modern times, which would alter the mother's history, of course. But that was the one thing about which I was absolutely steadfast: it was really important to me to write the book from the point of view of a teen whose mother lost family in the Holocaust. The Holocaust is in my blood; it's in my bones. It shaped my mother's life—and, as such, it has shaped mine. So, because I was firm about my protagonist's mother being a Holocaust survivor, I had to set *Camp* in the 1960s in order for the mother's history to be realistic.

In addition, I was a camper in the 1960s, so I know that period well enough to get the details right. If I would have written a current day camp story, not only would I have had to change the mother's history, but I would have had to immerse myself in modern camp culture. And although I'm not at all lazy, the thought of spending a chunk of time at a sleep-away camp today (so that the story would ring true) wasn't something I was eager to do.

Q: What was your greatest challenge in writing *Camp*? And what was your greatest satisfaction?

A: My greatest challenge in writing the book was keeping the story immediate while sharing Amy's thoughts and the interior voice that keeps playing in her head.

My greatest satisfaction was getting in touch with how it might have felt for my mother (and how it might feel for other immigrants who come to this country to escape war and terror) to build a new life in a foreign place. Writing

Camp gave me a chance to finally mourn fully for my mother. I cried while writing this story.

The dedication in the beginning of the book reads: "In loving memory of my mother, whose story I can only imagine." I hope *Camp* would have made her proud.

Q: What inspired the book's cover?

A: My publisher asked for my input when the designer was working on the cover, and after a couple of designs that I felt didn't accurately reflect the tone and story, the designer sent me one that became the actual cover. I'm really happy with the cover because it matches the image that was in my head while I was writing the book. *Camp* is a dark story (hence the barbed wire), and the title (especially with the barbed wire) is a double entendre. The main character is on a journey, as characters always are, so I wanted a path in an ominous camp setting. I think the cover designer did a great job.

Q: What is your writing process?

A: When I was writing *Camp*, I worked on it six days a week. Five of those days were "writing days." One day each week was a "thinking day." On "thinking days," I let the characters, the story, and my thoughts tumble in my mind, and I always had paper and pencil at hand. I took lots of long walks on those days, with a notepad and pencil in my fanny pack.

I was blessed with a writing mentor who lived in my neighborhood and with whom I often met on "thinking days." In addition, a writing instructor from the New School in New York City, where I had taken a novel writing course, met with me every few weeks to go over scenes and talk about what was working and what needed to be strengthened.

On each of my "writing days," I committed myself to creating two "keepable pages." That meant that sometimes I wrote five or six pages, over five or six or more hours, to get two "good pages." On some days, though, the scene and the voices just worked—and I got away from the computer after only a couple of hours.

Q: What's your favorite thing about being an author?

A: My favorite thing about being an author is creating characters and places that are as real to me as actual people and places. When I write, some of those characters become my good friends. I want to take care of them and protect them, yet they often take on lives of their own and make bad choices, which result in serious consequences.

I love hearing the characters' voices in my head when I'm writing strong scenes. And I love how my characters often lead me to reflect on my own life and the choices I've made. I think that the process of writing makes me a more observant, more appreciative, and more introspective person.

I love, too, that my novels have given me a platform as "the anti-bullying novelist." Now I have opportunities to speak widely about this issue.

Q: How did you develop your platform as "the anti-bullying novelist"?

A: I didn't intend to become an anti-bullying crusader; I just wrote what I hoped would be good, compelling novels. But because *Camp* is set in a sleep-away camp and my adult novel, *Danny's Mom*, is set in a high school, it was impossible not to write about bullying.

Early reviewers stated that I had created "really believable bullying scenes" and that "the mean girl voices are pitch perfect." The more I heard that, the more I realized that my novels could serve as springboards for conversations about bullying, and the more eager I became to use my books to make a difference: to keep anti-bullying conversations going so that, in concert with professionals in our communities, we will make our camps and schools kinder, gentler, more inclusive places for everyone.

Determined to get the word out about my mission to stop the bullying epidemic, I plunged into social media. People started to pay attention. The Holocaust Memorial & Tolerance Center of Nassau County (New York) selected *Camp* as a Book of the Month and then honored me with the Community Upstander Award. Radio personalities invited me to discuss my work on the air, which was great fun. Strong, positive reviews hit the internet, and bloggers asked for interviews. Those accolades and interviews led to lots of speaking engagements and to students, teachers, and book clubs finding out about *Camp*.

Now that bullying is finally part of our national dialogue, I know that if we all join the conversation, we will make our communities safer for everyone. I'm grateful that my books have given me this platform as "the anti-bullying novelist."

For more information, anti-bullying
resources, and additional interviews,
please visit the author at
www.authorelainewolf.com.